"What did Skip mean back there?" Kelsey interrupted, and Donna gave her a strange look.

"About what?"

"About people taking chances on the beach after dark, and your being lucky and finding them."

"Oh. That." Donna sighed and climbed over the rocks. "It happens sometimes, even when people are warned. It's like I told you, the lifeguards can't be on duty all the time. People think they're safe because they're only going in for a minute, just to wade or to take a quick dip. . . ."

"And they — "

"Drown," Donna finished. "We've had two drownings already this summer. It's not something we publicize. I mean, the last thing we want is for people to be afraid of this place."

"That's . . . horrible," Kelsey murmured. In spite of the hot sun, she shivered.

Also in the
Point Horror series:

April Fools
by Richie Tankersley Cusick

Trick or Treat
by Richie Tankersley Cusick

My Secret Admirer
by Carol Ellis

Beach Party
by R. L. Stine

Funhouse
by Diane Hoh

The Baby-sitter
by R. L. Stine

Teacher's Pet
by Richie Tankersley Cusick

Look out for:
The Boyfriend
by R. L. Stine

The Snowman
by R. L. Stine

The Invitation
by Diane Hoh

The Baby-sitter II
by R. L. Stine

The Girlfriend
by R. L. Stine

Mother's Helper
by A. Bates

Point Horror

THE LIFEGUARD

Richie Tankersley Cusick

Hippo Books
Scholastic Children's Books
London

Scholastic Children's Books,
Scholastic Publications Ltd,
7-9 Pratt Street, London NW1 0AE, UK

Scholastic Inc.,
730 Broadway, New York, NY 10003, USA

Scholastic Canada Ltd,
123 Newkirk Road, Richmond Hill,
Ontario, Canada L4C 3G5

Ashton Scholastic Pty Ltd,
P O Box 579, Gosford, New South Wales,
Australia

Ashton Scholastic Ltd,
Private Bag 1, Penrose, Auckland,
New Zealand

First published by Scholastic Inc, USA 1988
Published in the UK by Scholastic Publications Ltd, 1991

ISBN 0 590 76524 8

10 9 8 7 6 5

Printed by Cox & Wyman, Reading, Berks

to Dale and Ann ...
for your courage and inspiration

Prologue

The lifeguard picked his way carefully over the rocks, finally stopping to plunge his hands into the churning water.

There had been blood this time.

All the times before it had been so easy . . . so effortless . . . just that instant of surprise when they realized what was happening, and then everything over so quickly, so neat and clean, with hardly a struggle.

But this one was different.

This one had looked him right in the eyes, and begged for her life, and "Please," she had cried, over and over again, "Please don't kill me . . . please. . . ."

And he couldn't listen anymore, all that crying and pleading, couldn't look at her face, and he'd *had* to hit her . . . again . . . again . . . till finally she was quiet. . . .

He'd wanted to be gentle with *her*, of all people.

Because she'd trusted him . . . cared about him so much. . . .

But she'd *come* to him and *told* him that she knew, and she would have told others, and then they'd have put him away. . . .

No, he couldn't let that happen.

He had his reputation to think of.

After all . . . he was the lifeguard.

Chapter 1

"Don't struggle," the voice said. "Don't . . . it'll be easier if you don't struggle. . . ."

But the roaring came again, like it always did, that growing surge of indistinct sound and a scream, muffled, distant. . . .

"Don't struggle. . . ."

But she was struggling . . . great gasps of air from lungs bursting, and that split second, that terrifying instant of realization as strength gave out and water poured in, black and sickening and endless. . . .

"Don't. . . ." the voice was fading, as everything was fading, as her very life was fading . . . ending. . . .

"Oh, God, help me!"

Kelsey Tanner jolted upright, heart pounding, and her hands flew out, desperately seeking something to hold on to.

"Hey, you're okay. This old boat's been through a lot, but it's still pretty dependable."

She didn't know the boy beside her, but her hands were clamped down on his shoulders, and his eyes were so close that she could make out soft, green flecks beneath his lashes.

"Oh," she murmured and pulled away, conscious now of the rocking movement of the ferry and the flush creeping over her cheeks. "Oh . . . I didn't . . . I mean . . . I'm so sorry — "

The green eyes laughed at her. "Don't apologize. Women throw themselves at me all the time — I'm used to it. Look," he bent down to peer into her face. "You're still pretty pale — I'll get you some water."

"No, really, I feel fine. Don't go to any trouble — "

"No trouble," he grinned. "Be right back."

She gave a halfhearted nod and leaned back against the wall, watching him disappear down a stairway at the far end of the deck. *That dream again!* Kelsey shut her eyes against the memory, but the images began to gather like old familiar reruns, so she forced herself to stare at the vague outline of land in the distance. *Beverly Island.* She had never even heard of Beverly Island before, but Eric Connell, her mother's boyfriend, was coming here this summer to work on his plays and spend time with his kids, and he had invited Kelsey and Mrs. Tanner for a visit. Kelsey hadn't wanted to come — she'd had her heart set on going with her best friend to Jenny's family cabin in the mountains.

"His sons are lifeguards," Mom had tried to tempt her, "and his daughter can't wait to meet you — "

"We'll probably hate each other, and I'll probably hate the island, too!"

"You're going," Mom had said. And that was that.

Kelsey groaned and grabbed hold of the wall as the floor took a sudden slant beneath her feet.

Water. As far as she could see, choppy, gray water. An eternity of it.

"Here you go."

She slammed back against the railing as a hand reached out to steady her.

"Hey, easy — I really think you should sit down. Before you fall down." And it was him again, green eyes and wide, lazy smile, and strong hands guiding her back to the wooden bench, safely away from the sea.

"Just drink this and stay put. I'm a lifeguard, but I'd rather not have to rescue you this far from shore."

Kelsey's ears pricked up. "Lifeguard? Are you Eric Connell's son?"

For a moment Kelsey felt a twinge of uneasiness, looking into his eyes. He stared at her, his grin slowly fading. "No. Skip Rochford. But I know both his sons. Are you . . . a friend?"

"Sort of. I'm just visiting."

"Oh. Then I guess you haven't heard."

The uneasiness began to spread. "Heard what?"

Skip opened his mouth, but before he could answer, Mrs. Tanner rushed up, smiling as if she'd known him all her life.

"Isn't this boat great!" Mom waved her arms

in the air. "I can't believe we're really here, can you, Kelsey? No city for two whole weeks! I wanted you to feed the gulls with me, but you were having the best nap, and —"

At that, Skip glanced down at Kelsey's bent head. "You *are* better now, aren't you?"

"Yes," Kelsey said quickly. "Thanks again." She downed the last of the water and looked up to see her mother scrutinizing her.

"Something's wrong," Mrs. Tanner said flatly.

"No, Mom, it's just a little headache," Kelsey brushed it off. "I'm feeling much —"

"It was the dream again," Mom said, and Kelsey looked away, almost guiltily. "Oh, Kelsey, you haven't had it for such a long time now, I just —"

"It's all this," Kelsey's voice tightened. "The boat and all this water — you *know* how much I hate water, but you made me come anyway —" With a sharp intake of breath she folded her arms across her chest, trying to stop the violent shaking inside her.

"Well . . . if you're sure you're okay then," Skip said slowly, taking a step back. "I'd better get below. We'll be docking in a few minutes. See you on the island, huh?" He grinned and waved, vanishing into the crowds, but Kelsey closed her eyes and sighed.

"Kelsey," Mom said quietly. "Honey, I'm sorry. I thought it'd be good for you to have a vacation. Make new friends. I . . . guess I thought. . . ." her voice sank to a whisper and trembled, "maybe you could forget. . . ."

6

She trailed off, but Kelsey's mind raced on. *Forget?* How in the world would she ever be able to forget? When every sight of water reminded her? When the same nightmare kept coming back? When every time she looked in a mirror, the reminder was always there: her father's black eyes snapping back at her, her father's black hair, wavy and wild . . . *his* nose . . . *his* chin . . . *his* olive complexion . . . how could she ever forget when *he* wouldn't let her?

"Honey," Mom's hand settled lightly on Kelsey's head. "If you really hate it that much, you can call Jenny, and — "

"It's okay," Kelsey mumbled. "Come on — we'd better find our suitcases." As they joined the line near the exit, she even tried to laugh. "Well, at least Eric's kids have never met me, so I still have a chance of impressing *somebody*. What are their names again?"

Mom counted them off. "Let's see . . . there's Beth . . . the boys are Justin . . . and Neale. Eric said this vacation was really Beth's idea, that they see each other so seldom, she wanted to get everybody together again."

Kelsey mulled this over. "That's nice. She sounds sweet."

"Eric sure loves her — and Justin — he talks all the time about Justin's honors at school."

"What about Neale?"

Mom hesitated, a slight frown creasing her brow. "You know, I'm not really sure. Eric hardly ever talks about Neale. I might be wrong, but I *sense* something there. A holding back, maybe. I get the feeling he doesn't know Neale as well as the others."

"Maybe Neale's the problem child," Kelsey shrugged.

"Maybe," Mom mused. "Neale's the oldest, so it was probably hardest on him when their mother died. Whoops! Hang on, honey, I think we're going out!"

Kelsey braced herself for the stampede as they were sucked through the doors and down the gangplank. The first thing she saw was the pier, swarming with people and shops. The next thing she saw was Eric, fighting his way toward them.

Kelsey lifted her hand to wave.

And then she saw Eric's face and froze.

"Marjorie —" his voice cracked, and he grabbed them, held them close. "Marjorie, it's Beth." And then, as if both she and Kelsey were beyond understanding — "My daughter. She's missing."

Chapter 2

"What?" Mom's lips moved, marionettelike. "What — "

"The boys are with the search party now. I tried to get ahold of you, but — "

"We stopped off to see my parents." Mom looked dazed. "I never — "

Eric held up his hands. "I have to get back. We can talk on the way."

He shepherded them to a jeep, throwing their luggage in the back, and Kelsey climbed in with the suitcases.

"It happened three days ago. . . ." His shoulders hunched forward, fingers strained white on the wheel. "I should have kept tabs on her. She's only thirteen . . . but my work. . . ." His voice faltered "I just can't believe she's. . . ."

"Don't," Mom whispered. "Don't even think it."

"They found her sandals and a beach towel — covered with blood. . . ."

Kelsey looked away, suddenly feeling sick.

"Beth's a good swimmer, like her brothers. She knows the island, and she's not one to take risks."

"You don't think," Mom suggested gently, "that she . . . well . . . staged something . . . maybe ran away?"

"She was going out that night," Eric said. "With a local boy she really cared about. Skip Rochford."

"Skip. . . ." Kelsey murmured, but Eric didn't hear.

"The ferry only runs to the mainland twice a day. The last trip's at four, and Beth was still home then. I know because she yelled at me from the hall, and I looked at the clock on my desk."

"What about a private boat?" Mom was almost begging.

"They've already checked it out. Beth had no reason to leave here — she was *happy*."

Skip Rochford! Kelsey was sure that had been the name of the boy on the boat, but if that *was* the same Skip Rochford Eric was talking about, then why hadn't he seemed more upset? She pressed her nose against the fogged window, staring, when suddenly out of the rolling mist ahead something loomed up like a watchful animal. She leaned forward, frowning at the rocky horizon, at the black, ugly scars swelling against the hazy twilight, until the car turned into a driveway and stopped alongside a cottage.

The front door banged open immediately. "Dad?"

"Justin — has there been any — "

The shake of the boy's head stopped Eric in his tracks. "Nothing. They're still searching the cliffs, but. . . ." He looked at Kelsey and her mother standing awkwardly by the car.

"Justin," Eric murmured, "this is Marjorie and Kelsey. This is my son Justin."

"You look cold," Justin said softly. "Come on inside."

He stood a head taller than Kelsey, and although she knew he was about her age, his face had a mixture of solemnity and little-boyishness he would probably never outgrow. His hair was sun-tinted brown, silkily brushing his shoulders, and his eyes were big and brown and gentle, lowering shyly as she stared at him.

As Mom went into the house with Eric, Kelsey hesitated on the porch. "I'm . . . really sorry," she stammered.

His eyes raised slowly, meeting hers for a brief instant, then glancing away. "It's good you're here."

Kelsey nodded, squeezing past him into the living room. Justin's T-shirt smelled of salt and sand; his damp jeans clung tightly to his narrow hips. As he went to get their bags, Kelsey noticed a family photograph on the mantel — Eric, Justin, another boy half hidden in the shadows, and — she supposed — Beth, a pretty girl with dimples and long hair and a long red scarf around her neck.

"I'll show you your room if you want," Justin said behind her.

"Well . . . I don't know if we're staying — "

"Sure you're staying. Dad needs privacy for his work, so we have the cottage next door. Follow me."

He carried her suitcase across the yard and gave her a quick tour of the house.

"Neale and I are in here," Justin pointed to the first upstairs bedroom as they went past. "I guess he'll be coming back, now that it's getting dark. . . . Anyway, here's your room. You can use this first bed." He flipped on the light, and as she stepped across the threshold, her heart sank.

Beth was everywhere — in the decor, the clothes in the closet, the shoes under a chair. Kelsey swallowed hard and stared at the French doors next to her own bed, almost a whole wall of floor to ceiling glass.

"I don't think I can stay here."

Justin looked sympathetic. "Beth was really looking forward to meeting you. She'd thought up all kinds of things for you to do."

Kelsey walked slowly over to her bed, then saw something which made her stare. Propped against the pillows was an envelope with her name on it.

"What's this?" she asked softly.

Justin shrugged, a sad smile crossing his face. "Who knows . . . Beth was always leaving little surprises around for everybody."

Kelsey reached out and took the envelope between her fingers, sliding out the paper inside, staring down at the message for a long time:

Welcome, Kelsey! So glad you're here!
Love, Beth

"She didn't even know me," Kelsey murmured at last. She glanced up at Justin, who looked away. "Oh, Justin, I can't believe this is happening —"

"I can't, either." Justin shook his head, bewildered, like a child who didn't understand. "I keep waiting for her to walk in. . . ."

Kelsey sat down. "Do you . . . want to talk about it?"

"There's not much to tell," he sighed. "I didn't see Beth that day, but Neale saw her going home around three-thirty. She was supposed to meet a friend of mine that night. . . ."

Skip Rochford. . . . "You and Neale are lifeguards?"

"My friend Skip's one, too. There's two beaches on the island for swimming. West Beach is just down the hill from here. It goes about a mile along shore before it runs into the cliffs. The cliffs go another two miles — nobody's allowed to swim there — it's all sharp rocks and really deceiving. The cove's the most dangerous spot on the whole island. East Beach is on the other side of the island from here, but it's private."

"Who uses it?" Kelsey asked.

"The people who live there don't really use

the beach that much 'cause they have swimming pools. But they still want a lifeguard around for security."

"Which beach do you work on?"

"We switch off. East Beach only needs one lifeguard. It's small, and there's never much going on." He crossed to the French doors and stared out into the rainy darkness. "Three lifeguards . . . and not one of us helped Beth. . . ."

Kelsey was silent, turning the note over in her hand.

"They found some of her things at the cove," Justin said quietly. "Beth liked to take walks by herself . . . go off alone and think." He smiled, remembering. "Sometimes she'd come back with these stories — she wanted to be a writer — so half the time you never knew if what she said was real or imaginary."

Kelsey's throat ached, and she looked away.

"I don't know why she went there when she knew how dangerous it was." Justin lowered himself onto the other bed. "They think she probably fell, that she was hurt so bad, she never had a chance."

"What do you mean?"

"The cove. It's — " Justin broke off abruptly as a squeal of tires sounded beneath the windows, followed by the slamming of a car door. "There's Neale — maybe he's heard something — "

Kelsey followed slowly as Justin raced downstairs. Now she heard a new voice — deep and authoritative — cutting off the questions as they tumbled from Justin's mouth.

"They've called off the search till tomorrow, Justin, that's all I know."

"But — it'll be so cold out there again and — " Behind Justin's rising panic came the thud of a cabinet door, the chink of a coffee cup.

"Justin, why the hell are you worrying about the cold? You know as well as I do that she's dead."

Kelsey, frozen in the hall outside the kitchen, felt the sudden, suffocating silence . . . heard the gurgle of coffee being poured.

The deep voice sighed, gathering patience. "Look. You know what the cove's like. The tide comes in like a flood. Even if she *didn't* get smashed on the rocks, any one of those underwater caves could have sucked her down."

"I'm not giving up yet."

"Fine," the voice replied. "Where's Dad?"

"With Marjorie."

"Oh, hell, are *they* here?"

There was no mistaking the disgust in the voice, and Kelsey cringed back against the wall. She had never heard such coldness, such lack of feeling, and an inexplicable stab of fear went through her. She had no desire to meet Neale, but before she could leave, Eric and Mom rushed through the door.

Kelsey, slipping in after them, got her first look at Neale Connell and felt her heart squeeze into her throat.

He was much taller than Justin — so lean

and tan in just the faded jeans he wore that he seemed like a shadow lurking in the far corner of the kitchen. He tipped his coffee cup to his lips, casual and unhurried, yet from across the room Kelsey knew he had seen her. He was watching her even now, she could feel it — those dark, dark eyes in cool appraisal over the rim of his cup; the peculiar light they had, like some cat, calmly assessing his prey. . . .

Kelsey averted her eyes, but not before noticing his thick black hair, the firm set of his jaw, the high cheekbones, the sinewy curve to his upper arms. He lowered the cup, still watching her, and she moved closer to Justin.

Eric pressed his fists to his eyes. "We have to do *something* — "

"There's nothing else we can do," said Neale. He poured himself another cup of coffee. "There's nothing anyone can do. They've questioned everyone they can think of. Nobody saw her, and nobody knows anything. Or so they say."

"No," Eric said quietly. "I can't accept that."

Neale shifted and cleared his throat. "Dad . . . I think you're gonna have to."

Eric stared back at him. "Wasn't there anything else Skip could remember?"

"I wouldn't count on Skip for anything," Neale said acidly.

"He still says he came by to get Beth at six, and she wasn't here," Justin broke in.

"But I was right next door," Eric said. "Why didn't he tell *me* Beth wasn't here?"

"He did, Dad," Justin said softly. "Don't

you remember? He said he yelled in at the door, but you were typing, and he didn't want to interrupt you."

Eric looked exhausted. "Yes, you're right . . . I'm like that when I'm working . . . not always quite aware. . . ."

Neale pushed himself slowly away from the counter. "Why don't you get some sleep? If we hear anything, we'll wake you."

"Yes," Eric said absently. "I don't believe you've met — Neale, this is Marjorie and Kelsey."

Neale mumbled something unintelligible and Kelsey nodded, escaping gratefully to the hall. She shook her head, trying to clear it, and started slowly upstairs, the floorboards groaning beneath her footsteps. The only upstairs light on was the one in Beth's room. . . .

Beth's. . . .

Kelsey hesitated in the doorway. Yes, Beth was everywhere, sweet and thoughtful, and somehow, very much alive. . . .

Rubbing the sudden chill from her arms, Kelsey reached into the closet for a hanger, and was startled when a piece of paper fell onto the floor. She leaned down and picked it up, a puzzled smile on her face as she read:

> *Kelsey,*
> *I know we will be great friends!*
> *Love, Beth.*

How special, Kelsey thought . . . so considerate, so accepting. . . . Trusting, Kelsey decided. Beth must have been so trusting. . . .

It was so cold in here. Kelsey tried to close the window over her bed, but it wouldn't budge. Pulling harder, she felt her earring snag on her sleeve and drop down behind the headboard. Easing onto her stomach, she reached under the bed and accidentally knocked her pillow onto the floor.

There beside her where her pillow had been, was a small piece of folded notepaper.

Kelsey smiled, propping herself on her elbows as she unfolded it. Beth must have put it there, for her to find when she went to sleep tonight —

The smile froze on Kelsey's face.

The writing blurred, and her hands began to shake.

Kelsey,
*   I think someone is going to kill me.*

Chapter 3

It was a joke, of course. It had to be.

Kelsey stared at the crumpled paper on the nightstand where she'd tossed it, and Justin's words rang again and again in her head — *"Beth was always leaving little surprises around for everybody. . . ."*

Of course it was a joke.

Except Beth was missing, and it wasn't funny.

Kelsey jumped as a door slammed downstairs. She heard Justin in the hallway and just managed to grab the note as he came into the room.

"I'm supposed to tell you to get some sleep," he said softly, smiling. "I'll be downstairs if you need anything."

"Thanks, but if you have stuff to do, go ahead."

"No, I'll be downstairs," he said again. "I'm not going anywhere."

What else *could* he do, Kelsey thought sadly, but wait. After he'd left, she pulled the note out again, studying the handwriting. At first glance it had looked the same as the other notes, but now she could see that it wasn't quite so neat — as if this note had been written in a great hurry.

What should I do? Everyone was so upset already, so convinced that Beth's disappearance was an accident. And hadn't Justin said how Beth loved going off alone to dream? If Kelsey presented this note now, a whole new set of horrible possibilities would open up. And for what? One piece of paper that might only be some fantasy in Beth's mind. . . . *"Half the time you never knew if what she said was real or imaginary."* Just a story, probably. *But why was the note addressed to me?*

Suddenly Kelsey had an idea. She'd call Jenny. Jenny would know what to do.

Jamming the note into the pocket of her robe, Kelsey let herself out into the hall. Downstairs the TV blared and cupboard doors slammed, so she figured Justin was occupied, at least for a while. She wished she could just go down and ask him where the phone was, but if it was in the same room with him then he'd be able to hear everything she was saying. No, better to find an extension.

Kelsey made a futile search of the upstairs. Frustrated, she started back into her room to go take a shower, when she heard the phone ring from below. Well, at least it existed *somewhere* — now if only she could get to it tomorrow without anyone hearing. . . .

When she finally stepped out of the shower,

the house was silent. Kelsey buttoned her nightgown and opened the bathroom door.

Funny . . . I could have sworn I left the light on. . . .

Kelsey froze in the unexpected blackness. She ran her palms over the wall, searching for a light switch, then took several steps forward, groping with outstretched hands through the darkness. Suppose Justin had gone out and left her there, and that note — *that note* — still hidden in her robe, and Beth's bed so empty beside her own. . . .

Suppose Beth had come back.

Suppose Beth was even now curled up in her bed . . . in the dark . . . watching her. . . .

"Oh, God — " Kelsey pitched forward onto a mattress, and in a terror-filled instant, clawed for the lamp, filling the room with soft, safe light.

The room was the same. And she was alone.

Breathing a sigh of relief, she switched off the light again, tossed her robe across her feet, and huddled down under the covers. She could feel her eyes drooping . . . the room receding around her, a soft whirl of blackness, a soft murmur of sound . . . like surf . . . the faraway sighing of the sea. . . .

"Don't struggle," the voice said . . . "Don't . . . it'll be easier if you don't struggle. . . ."

But the roaring came again like it always did, that growing surge of indistinct sound and a scream, muffled, distant —

"Don't . . . struggle. . . ."

But she was struggling . . . great gasps of

air from lungs bursting and that split second, that terrifying instant of realization as strength gave out and water poured in, black and sickening and endless ... always endless. ...

"Don't. ..." the voice was fading again, and this time the face flashed, only a second, wavy in the water, eyes staring, saying her name, Kelsey, Kelsey ... don't struggle ... as everything was fading, as her very life was fading ... ending. ...

"Dad! Help me! Oh, please, somebody help!"

She was standing beside her bed, only she didn't remember climbing out — just standing there with her arms wrapped around herself, shaking, freezing, just slipped out of a nightmare —

She sobbed and raised her eyes in the dark, put her palms flat against the French doors —

And saw the black eyes staring back at her from the other side.

Kelsey wasn't sure what happened next. In a daze, she heard screaming — doors banging and feet running, and suddenly a deep voice, furious, as the French doors burst open.

"What the hell's going on!"

And then another voice spoke, quiet and very close, "I think she was having a nightmare — you shouldn't have scared her like that."

"Scared her! Beth's dead out there somewhere, it's nearly two in the morning, and I hear a scream — and I'm supposed to stop and think about not *scaring* someone — "

"Well, you knew *I* was here, didn't you?"

"With no lights on? I didn't think *anyone* was here!"

"You should have had your key," the quiet voice said.

"You should have left a door unlocked."

The voices, the room, the light — everything was pulling back into place at last. To Kelsey's surprise she saw Justin's arm around her shoulders, and then, framed in the French doors, she saw Neale.

He looked as if he hated her.

Dropping her eyes, Kelsey stammered, "Oh . . . I thought — "

"It's okay, he was just trying to get in. He forgot his key, and our room opens onto the deck like this one." Justin gave her a little shake and smiled. "You must have had a nightmare. Think you can get back to sleep?"

Kelsey nodded, avoiding Neale's stare. "Yes, I think so. I'm really sorry — I — "

"Don't worry about it. Just get some rest, okay?"

"Okay." Neale was so dark there in the doorway, his eyes so black, so piercing. He made her feel trapped, as if he could see through walls and around corners and in the dark.

"Good-night, then." Justin stood up, smiling, and she couldn't help smiling back.

"Good-night. And I'm really sorry."

Neale fastened the doors and followed his brother out of the room, but though Kelsey slid right into bed again, she couldn't sleep. She lay awake long after the voices in the next room had stopped, and when the room finally began to lighten, she got up at once. Throwing on shorts and a T-shirt, she crept downstairs and let herself out. If she was going to be stuck here, she might as well see what there was to do.

The beach was deserted at this early hour. Kelsey walked to the water's edge and stared out over the waves. She didn't swim anymore since the accident, and a cold hatred had replaced her love of the water. Now, as she turned away from it, she fought back tears and carefully trained her eyes on the sand and its scatterings of shells and driftwood.

A lifeguard station loomed up ahead of her, a dark skeleton against lavender daybreak. She paused for a minute, leaning her head against the stilted legs of the wooden tower, and took a deep breath, listening to the gulls, the rumble of the surf. Strange that there wasn't another soul on the whole beach . . . yet somehow, she felt like she wasn't alone. . . .

Suppressing a shudder, Kelsey hurried on. The sun was higher now, and as the sky paled around her, something in the distance took on sudden shape and substance, separating itself from the gloom and stopping her midstride.

She had seen it yesterday from the jeep window. Only now it was even closer. And even more menacing.

The craggy wall of rock rose steeply against the horizon, clawing ragged holes in the dawn, yet as she stared, Kelsey began to see that it wasn't a sheer wall at all — rather a mass of sharp cliffs and oversized boulders lumped together, leaning far out into the sea. They seemed so cruel, somehow, as if deep, deep down, below the ugly scars and ridges, there was a mind, slow and cunning, aware of everything. Glancing nervously around, Kelsey went on.

The beach began to disappear. One moment it was clutching the rocks, and then it tapered off, tunneling beneath a low stone overhang as the cliffs swallowed it whole. Kelsey stopped, uncertain. Surely there must be another pathway. . . .

Gasping, she whirled, her eyes darting nervously over the empty beach behind her. Empty. . . .

And yet she'd had that feeling again . . . that someone was watching her.

Shading her eyes, she scanned the crags above. The sun, inching steadily higher, dissolved the last of the shadows and drenched the rocks golden, and as Kelsey squinted against the glare, she noticed one peak pulling away from the others, standing out from the mass of rocks as if it didn't really belong. She walked closer, eyes glued to the peculiar shape, and then a smile spread over her face.

"A lighthouse!"

In the sunlight the tall tower stood out easily from its surroundings, and Kelsey's eyes swept the incline, looking for a way up. She threaded her way behind the dunes, through sparse patches of trees growing back from the sand, skirting the cliffs. To her delight she discovered a narrow road carved into the side of the cliff, leading upwards, disappearing into the jagged spears of rock. A high iron gate had been erected across the entrance — nearly twelve feet tall, she guessed — and the gate was open. Kelsey frowned and went closer. The chain that secured the gate was swinging free, the huge iron padlock unhinged. Taking a deep breath, she squeezed between the gate and the rocks and started up.

It seemed to take forever. Muscles aching, she followed the tedious twists and turns, shivering as the wind grew wilder, as the rocks pressed unnaturally close. Then without any warning, the lighthouse was standing just ten feet away.

It looked like an oversized headstone.

As Kelsey stared up at its dingy, crumbling walls, her excitement turned to disappointment. It was a dull, mottled color, rust and mildew trailing up the once-white stone, and it wasn't straight as it had appeared below, but rather seemed to lean like the cliffs, out over the water. Kelsey let her eyes rove up, up, to the actual light tower atop the house. It looked so spooky perched up there all alone, walls and windows disintegrated from their frameworks, the encircling deck rotted away to a few splintered railings. *It probably doesn't even have a floor anymore . . . or stairs . . . only ghosts. . . .*

Giving herself a firm mental shake, Kelsey walked toward the entrance. It was so isolated up here . . . so forgotten. . . . She reached out toward the lighthouse door and gave it a shove.

She didn't expect it to open.

She didn't expect to fall across the threshold and sprawl facedown in the dirt and sand, scrabbling madly to tear the sticky cobwebs from her face. . . .

And she didn't expect the laugh.

The high, shrill, singsong laugh that rose up from the depths of the lighthouse and echoed again and again from a face she couldn't see.

Chapter 4

In her panic Kelsey fell against the door, jamming it shut, but as the senseless laughter faded around her, she jerked at the latch and stumbled out into the deserted yard. As the wind forced her back toward the road, she spun around to gaze back at the lighthouse.

The man was right behind her.

With a scream, Kelsey jumped back, eyes riveted helplessly on his ghastly appearance. He seemed a giant skeleton, tattered clothes billowing from his lanky frame, a moth-eaten cap pulled low upon his brow. He was dressed like a fisherman, yet the hands that dangled from his frayed cuffs looked like they could crush effortlessly with a touch. But it was his face — sun-wrinkled, wind-weathered — that filled her with such loathing. The leathery skin was covered with moles, and where his right eye should have been there was only a filthy black patch. His left eye, narrowed and slanted, was tinged with yellow, and spit clung to the sprouting of whiskers on his chin.

Kelsey took another step back, ready to run.

"What you doing here, girl? Hmmm?" The voice was brittle, the laugh a shrill, thin cackle that left him gasping for breath.

Swallowing hard, Kelsey glanced toward the road.

"You a tourist?" The one eye pinned her where she stood, and he cocked his head. "You come to swim? Or die maybe?" He chuckled at her look of horror, shaking his head from side to side. "Funny things happen to girls swimming round here. Maybe you hear about these things, hmmm?" He took a wobbly step toward her, and Kelsey realized she couldn't move at all, she was too terrified. "You think I hurt you, girl? I won't hurt you. Isaac don't hurt nobody. See?" He groaned and lowered himself to the ground, joints popping. "I sit down. Here. Can't chase you if I'm sitting now, can I?"

Kelsey watched him, a strange curiosity slowly replacing her fear. If only he wouldn't stare at her with that eye. . . .

"So," he said. "You come to swim?"

Kelsey felt her lips move. "I don't like to swim."

"No?" His scraggly brows drew together. "But let me see . . . you don't live around here 'cause I never seen you. So you gotta be a tourist. And tourists come to swim."

"I don't like to swim," Kelsey said again. "I don't like water."

The old man slapped his leg, a fine spray of saliva flying from his mouth as he laughed loudly. "You're funny, girl! You come to the beach and you don't like to swim. You come to the island and you don't like water! What you gonna do?" He rocked back a little, his eye a thoughtful slit as it looked her up and down. "You smart girl, not to swim, maybe. Maybe stay alive that way."

A chill snaked its way up her spine, and Kelsey moved her feet, testing the ground behind her.

"But wait — I *did* see you before. You got off the boat yesterday."

Kelsey knew if she had seen the old man yesterday she would never have forgotten that face. She frowned and saw that he was laughing at her.

"You don't see me, but I see you." The grizzled head bobbed slowly. "Isaac sees a lot of things."

One step back. "What . . . what do you mean by that?"

He lay one finger along his upper lip, smugly considering. "Ever hear of the ninth day, girl?"

Kelsey shook her head.

"When a person be drowned, his body will float on the ninth day. Except this body ain't a he. And it ain't never gonna have a chance to float."

Kelsey stared at him, her legs turned to rubber beneath her. "I . . . I don't know what you're talking about. You're just trying to scare me — "

He gave a high-pitched chuckle. "Me? Scare a nice little girl like you? Isaac just tells the truth; you should listen to old Isaac."

"I should report you!"

"Report me?" he breathed in, his face mocking. "Well, now, I see I was wrong about you, wasn't I?"

"Wrong about what?"

"I thought you be a smart girl. I thought you listen to the truth."

"You tried to scare me back there, and it wasn't funny —"

"You're right, girl, it wasn't." His grin faded, lips settling into a thin, serious line. "It wasn't funny. And it wasn't me."

A gust of wind whined around the lighthouse, and Kelsey glanced toward the tower, suddenly cold. "What do you mean it wasn't you? I *heard* you! You were watching me!"

For several moments he regarded her passively, his lips finally curling into a humorless smile. "Don't believe everything you see, girl. Folks ain't always what they seem to be."

Kelsey turned her back on him and started walking, fearfully conscious now of the old man lumbering to his feet.

"You remember what I say!" he shouted. "You remember, and you have a care! There's evil all around you, closing you in! It's *got* you! Anytime it wants you, it's *got* you —"

She heard him running now, stumbling after her, and in terror she veered off the road, scrambling over a ledge, praying for a foothold. The cliff went almost straight down. Trying not to look, she felt her way backward over the rocks when she heard a sharp whistle above. The old man was at the edge of the cliff, grinning down at her, his eye patch like a dark scab on the side of his face.

Gasping, Kelsey scrabbled down another few feet, clutching at anything she could find. She didn't even see the loose stone that turned her foot and threw her off balance. Groping wildly at an overhang of brush, she felt the weeds come loose in her hands, the searing pain as her body slid down the cliff toward the sea below.

There wasn't even time to scream.

Shutting her eyes, she braced herself for the impact, the cold water . . . *"anytime it wants you it's got you . . . got you. . . ."*

"I've got you!"

The voice was right in her ear, and arms, strong and warm and solid, tight around her body. . . .

"What the *hell* do you think you're doing?"

Kelsey's eyes flew open. Neale's face was just inches from her own, his body stretched out beneath hers.

"I . . . that man was chasing me — " Kelsey struggled in his grasp, but Neale's arms were like steel. With one heave he pushed her away, and she scrambled up. "I slipped — that man — "

"Don't you know you could have been *killed!*" He was positively seething, and Kelsey stepped back, tripping over her own feet. "*Nobody* climbs on those rocks, you understand? Nobody! If anything had happened to you, there wouldn't have been anyone around to help you!"

"Well . . . well, *you* were here!"

Neale was fighting for control. "There's no

telling what could happen this far from the main beach — you could have broken something or speared yourself on the rocks. Not to mention drowning. Or sharks."

"Sharks! But — the water's too shallow — "

"How do you know? Have you been in?"

"Well — no — but — I just thought — "

"You just thought," he glowered at her. "Sharks don't *need* deep water to rip you apart — three feet would do them just fine."

Kelsey flushed with embarrassment. "But that man — he was coming after me and — " She was babbling and pointing at the same time, and as Neale followed the direction of her arm, his eyes grew even darker.

"You were up *there?* You went to the *lighthouse?*" He was incredulous. "How the hell did you get up there?"

"Through — up the road — "

"The road! What's the matter with you, can't you read?"

"Read what?" His anger was frightening her again, and she grew defensive. "I don't know what you're talking about — " She broke off, eyes widening, as he grabbed her and began pulling her around the side of the cliff. When they finally reached the road, he pushed her so roughly towards the gate that she nearly went sprawling.

"Read it," he ordered.

Kelsey looked where he pointed, and she gasped.

The gate was shut. And locked.

And the sign posted on it had big, bold

letters that could have been seen half a mile away: PRIVATE ROAD DANGER POSITIVELY NO TRESPASSING.

"I. . . ." Her lips moved, the color draining from her face. "I . . . that wasn't there before."

"It's always there. It's been there for the whole summer. And the summer before this one."

"Look, I'm not lying! You can think what you want, but that sign wasn't there! I swear it! Someone must have — "

"What?" The black eyes challenged her.

"Must have moved it," she finished lamely. "Look, I know it sounds stupid, but — "

"You're right. It sounds stupid."

"The sign wasn't there," Kelsey snapped. "And what about that crazy old man up there who tried to chase me down the cliff? What about him spying on me, what about that? *He* probably took down the sign — I felt him watching me even before I went up the road!"

"What crazy old man?" Neale sighed.

"Don't tell me I'm making him up, too," Kelsey jerked her chin towards the lighthouse. "He was hiding up there and tried to scare me with that disgusting eye patch — "

"Oh," Neale nodded, shrugging his shoulders. "Old Isaac. Sleeping off another hangover, probably. You *should* have been scared — maybe that'll put some sense into you."

"Don't talk to me like that," Kelsey said, hands clenching at her sides. "That old man could have taken down the sign, and you know it. Anyone could have taken it down."

Neale went over to the sign and grabbed the length of chain woven neatly between the metal rails. "See this? This is to keep nosy people like you out of here. The gate stays locked all the time. Only the lifeguards have keys to it." He pulled a ring from his pocket, separating one heavy blue key from all the others.

Kelsey stared at him, at the padlock anchoring the chain, at the empty road on the other side of the gate. "It wasn't locked," she mumbled. "I didn't imagine it —"

"Okay. A mirage, right? Or you walked right through it, maybe?" For several long moments Neale stared at her, a muscle working in his jaw. "Okay," he said at last. "Come with me."

Kelsey shrank away as he grabbed her arm again and began dragging her back around the cliff. When they reached the overhang where the beach disappeared, Neale ducked under, leaving her no choice but to go with him. There was a brief moment of darkness as they wound through a low stone tunnel, but almost immediately they went up an incline out into the sun.

They were on a smaller beach, penned by towering cliffs on three sides, the ocean on the other. Only this beach was different from the one she had seen that morning. Kelsey stared at the jagged rocks sticking out of the water along the shore, at the spikes of stone edging her in all around, all black and coated with slime. The wind screamed around them, beating the low tide into a frenzied boil. And those awful, razor-edged rocks. As black as death.

Kelsey's stomach tightened with some sense of imminent danger. The water was too close here — too wild — and those boats, rocking slowly on the waves beyond the first outcrop of sawtoothed rocks . . . those boats just heaving up and down . . . up and down. . . .

"What are they doing out there?" Kelsey wanted to run from them. "They're too close to the rocks. Shouldn't you warn them?"

Neale looked down at her, his face hard. "They're looking for Beth. They found her things on that ledge over there."

Kelsey didn't want to look, yet felt her eyes following the point of his finger. The ledge was only partway up the cliff, easily accessible, and surrounded by water that appeared fairly shallow.

"It's not so deep now," Neale went on, and Kelsey jumped as if he had read her mind. "You could wade in it as long as the current doesn't slam you up against those rocks. But later . . . when the tide comes in. . . ." His voice dropped, and Kelsey stepped away from him. "Should I go on?" Neale asked in mock politeness.

"I don't like it here," Kelsey forced some authority into her voice that she didn't feel. "I'm going back."

"Suit yourself. It's not fun to think about. Being trapped here."

Kelsey turned on her heel and fought down the urge to run. Neale had done this to her on purpose, and she didn't know what he was trying to prove anyway. He didn't seem to be taking his sister's death very hard, and he *certainly* didn't seem to like *her*. Kelsey wondered if Neale cared about anything. She ducked through the tunnel, falling gratefully out into the daylight at the other end. She didn't know if he was following or not as she hurried back along the beach. To her relief there were other people out now, the sounds of distant shouting and laughter. Kelsey quickened her pace. She wouldn't let Neale upset her; she'd just try to stay out of his way and —

"Look out!"

The dog came out of nowhere, and as it leaned its huge paws on Kelsey's shoulders, she heard shouting from all directions.

"Donna, you know the rules! No dogs on the beach!"

"I know the rules, Neale Connell! He broke his chain! What do you want me to do?"

"Hey, it's okay — he won't hurt you!"

As three people converged on her all at once, Kelsey managed to free herself from the dog's embrace.

"Gosh, I'm really sorry — I hope Rex didn't scare you — Oh! Are you Kelsey? I'm Donna Westin — I heard you were here for a visit." The blonde girl now paused for breath and pumped Kelsey's hand warmly, a contagious smile lighting up her whole pixieish face. Kelsey smiled back, but before she could reassure the girl, Donna rushed on. "Skip here told me he met you — now we're *all* practically neighbors — only some of us are more sociable than others." She glared at Neale, who didn't seem at all perturbed.

Kelsey looked into Skip's green eyes and felt her own smile widen. "Hi."

"You should keep better company." Skip grinned. "Having fun?"

Kelsey had forgotten all about Neale, but now he spoke up and moved out from behind her.

"She seems to think that one death's not enough excitement around here."

Donna gasped, and the air grew electrically still. "God, Neale . . . that's a terrible thing to say — "

Neal gazed past Donna to Skip, who was looking at the ground. "I've noticed Skip doesn't seem to be too torn up about anything — "

"Knock it off, Neale," Skip said quietly.

"That's not fair, Neale, and you — " Donna began, but Skip cut her off.

"I was only meeting Beth. To talk. We weren't going to run away together, for — "

"Don't argue with him, Skip, he's just upset, he's — "

"I know what you think of me, Neale." Skip's voice lowered, and his green eyes fixed themselves on Neale's face. "I know you don't like me, and I really don't care. But if you're looking for a suspect, the sheriff's already given me the third degree, and I'm still out on the streets. And in case you haven't noticed, I'm not even handcuffed!"

"Not that it would matter," Neale retorted. "Your father'd just buy your way out of it."

Skip made a sudden move, but Donna thrust herself between them, her hands on Skip's chest.

"Stop it! You're just *upset*, Neale — *anybody* would be! We're *sorry* — *we're all sorry* — so don't say anything else. You, either, Skip, just keep *quiet!*"

Kelsey saw Neale's eyes, the livid set of his face, and a shiver of apprehension went through her as he slowly, slowly drew himself back.

"Get your damn dog off the beach," he muttered.

They watched him walk away, and then Skip cupped his hands to his mouth, throwing a shout straight at Neale's back.

"She can do whatever she wants as long as I'm around — *I own this beach!*"

Chapter 5

"Not the greatest introduction," Donna said ruefully. "I'm really sorry about all that."

"It's not your fault," Kelsey threw her a tight smile. "I think maybe I'm starting to get used to him."

"Yeah, well, good luck."

They looked at one another and burst out laughing, and Skip glanced down at his watch.

"Look, I've got to run — I'm on duty. Just ignore him, Kelsey, that's what we do." He tipped his baseball cap. "Ladies . . . I trust you'll have the pleasure of my company again?"

"If you're lucky," Donna retorted, and he gave them a jaunty wave as he trotted up the beach.

"So," Donna was all smiles again. "How about some breakfast? I know a great place for cinnamon rolls."

"Well. . . ." Kelsey shaded her eyes and peered off through the gathering crowds. "I didn't tell anyone I was leaving, and I really don't know what the situation is back at the house — "

"I understand." Donna's face was sympathetic, and Kelsey felt comfortably drawn to her. "It must be awful for you, showing up in the middle of everything. Sure you wouldn't go for one little roll?"

She looked so beseeching that Kelsey laughed and gave in. "To tell the truth, I don't really want to go back to the cottage now. Neale really hates us being there, I think."

"Oh . . . Neale." Donna nodded and whistled to her dog. "Neale's like that about everything. He's not real popular around here."

"What was all that about between him and Skip just now?" She fell into step with Donna along the shore.

"Who ever knows, with Neale . . . ?" Donna shook her head. "Skip was supposed to meet Beth that night, so I guess Neale thinks Skip can clear up the mystery somehow." Donna steered her away from the beach through the trees. "Come on, the diner's this way."

Kelsey straggled up the hillside, stopping to catch her breath as she saw the old building with its WEST DINER sign.

"Fancy, huh?" Donna swept long hair back from her face and waited for Kelsey to catch up. "The busiest part of the beach is farther down, past your cottage. That's where everyone really hangs out. But this place doesn't have so many tourists. No offense." Winking mischievously, she tied Rex to a post by the door and pulled Kelsey inside.

"Aren't you afraid to leave him?" Kelsey asked as Donna nudged her into a booth by the window.

"Kelsey, it's so safe on this island, it's positively boring." Donna gave the menu a cursory glance. "We get *some* important people here, like Eric, of course. Artists. Writers. People who rent for the summer. The others are tourists — they only come for the day."

Kelsey unfolded her napkin. "How come the media isn't beating down Eric's door? People must know what's happened, and he's well-known."

"Yeah, but that's where Skip's father comes in. Skip's grandmother was Beverly, if that tells you anything."

"Beverly?" Kelsey stared at her, totally baffled, and Donna leaned across the table, her face animated.

"Beverly Island."

"Oh!" Kelsey's eyes widened. "You mean *that* Beverly?"

"That Beverly!" Donna looked pleased with herself and bounced back against the torn upholstery. "Well, I can't actually remember *which* grandmother, but it was one of them. The island's been in the family for generations."

"So when he said he owned the beach, he wasn't kidding." Kelsey let it all sink in, shaking her head. "Is that why Neale doesn't like him?"

"Well, let's face it, Skip's not very discreet about his position around here. Like I was say-

ing about his father — Eric didn't want re-
porters around, so Mr. Rochford took care of it.
He's got money and power, and what he says
goes. Skip usually gets what he wants." Donna
greeted the waitress and ordered coffee and
rolls for two. "I don't think Neale liked Skip
hanging around Beth. She had kind of a crush
on him."

"Maybe he's just an overprotective big
brother," Kelsey suggested.

Donna shook her head. "They were all stuck
in boarding schools most of the year. And sum-
mers were spent with relatives and friends
'cause Eric never had the time. That's what
Skip told me, anyway." Donna sat back as the
waitress placed a steaming mug of coffee in
front of her. "Eric farmed them all out after
their mother died . . . they never really saw each
other while they were growing up."

"How does Skip know all this?"

"He and Justin have roomed together at
school the last few years. They're best friends
— swim team, honors, all that good stuff."

"Maybe that's when the friction with Neale
and Skip started — "

"Uhh-uh." Donna shook her head and reached
for the plate between them. "Neale wasn't at
the same school. Skip didn't even know Justin
had a brother — Justin never mentioned him."

"That's weird. . . ."

"Yeah, especially 'cause they're only a year
apart, so it's funny that they were always in
different schools."

Kelsey chewed slowly on a lump of cinnamon roll. "Maybe they never got along, and Eric had to keep them separated."

Donna frowned, staring thoughtfully into her cup. "It's funny about Neale — I've never heard anyone say anything about him. It's almost like they don't *know* anything about him. Or they *do* know something but it's horrible and they're trying to keep it a big, dark secret." Kelsey shifted uncomfortably in her seat, and Donna grinned. "You're probably right; they probably just didn't get along. Neale's so sneaky, and Justin's so sweet. Girls always mob the lifeguards, but Justin's so shy! Not like Skip." Donna flushed.

"Is Skip . . . your boyfriend?"

There was mild hopelessness in Donna's eyes. "We've grown up together, but I don't think he's ever noticed I'm not the kid down the road anymore."

"Maybe you should go out with Neale," Kelsey deadpanned. "Maybe Skip would notice that."

Donna laughed and reached for another roll. "Neale's so creepy. Like last summer he just showed up on the island. I don't even think Justin knew he was coming."

"So Justin was here?"

"Yeah, he and Skip have been lifeguards here for the past few years. Neale stayed someplace down the beach and kept to himself. I never saw him much — at least not till after the drowning."

"Drowning?" Kelsey's ears pricked up, her skin going cold.

"It was really sad," Donna's voice lowered, "especially 'cause Rebecca was a friend of ours. She was a lifeguard, too — she drowned trying to rescue someone."

Kelsey stared hard at the table, the roll like a rock in the pit of her stomach. "How horrible . . . did the other person drown, too?" She looked up but Donna was gazing out the window, a puzzled expression on her face.

"That's the strange thing," Donna said slowly. "There's a phone at each lifeguard station. When any of them has an emergency they take their phone off the hook — that alerts the other lifeguards and the paramedics."

"Did . . . didn't anybody come?"

"Oh, they came all right. But by the time Skip and Justin got to her, she was already dead. And there wasn't anyone else in the water."

"What . . . do you mean?"

"I mean nobody else was out there. Nobody ever washed up on the beach, and no one was ever reported missing. Rebecca was all alone."

Kelsey reached mechanically for her coffee cup, for some bit of leftover warmth to quell the chill she felt inside.

"It was just about time for the beach to close, and there weren't many people around," Donna sighed. "Just some kids on their way home."

"Well, surely they saw something?"

"They said they heard someone yelling for help, and saw splashing around in the water, like someone was in trouble, but it was too far away to make out. Anyway, nobody believed them. Everyone said it was probably just seagulls, and when nothing ever turned up, well. . . ."

Kelsey closed her eyes, not wanting to hear any more.

"That's when Neale became a lifeguard — he took over Rebecca's job." Donna shook her head with a derisive laugh. "I can't believe I'd forgotten about all that. It was just about this time last year."

Chapter 6

"Mom!"

Kelsey paused, listening, relieved when she heard a door open upstairs and the rapid thud of feet down the hall.

"Kelsey — where on earth have you been? I've had Justin looking everywhere for you, but he had to go to work — "

"Mom, I'm fine, I just went for a walk. Has anyone heard anything?"

Mom shook her head, running one hand through disheveled hair. "No, honey, nothing. I sure could use some coffee — want to join me?"

Kelsey poured the coffee, trying to think where to start. Donna . . . the old man at the lighthouse . . . her feeling of being watched on the beach . . . *the note*. . . . With everything else that had happened that morning, it had been pushed completely from her mind. Now she frowned, wondering what to do, and lowered herself into a chair.

"You remember the guy on the boat yesterday? I saw him on the beach this morning, and this girl — Donna — is a friend of his and Justin's. We went and had some breakfast and talked."

"That's nice," Mom said, but her look was distracted. "Kelsey, they're calling off the search after today. They're convinced Beth fell and drowned, and they don't think they'll ever find her."

"Oh, Mom. . . ."

"Eric wants me to stay."

"I understand."

"Now look, you can call Jenny and see if you can still go with her folks to the mountains and — "

"Mom, I can't leave now." Kelsey scooted forward, her voice urgent. "I just . . . wouldn't feel right about it."

Mom sighed and pulled her close in a hug. "Do you think you can manage on your own? Try to have a good time in spite of everything? I know it won't be much of a vacation, and Eric thinks you might be better off. . . ."

"Tell Eric not to worry. I'm really okay. I just wish I could help."

"We all wish that, honey. But no one can do anything because no one *knows* anything. There's no proof. . . ." She lowered her voice again and it trembled. "You just can't give up, can you, if there's no proof . . . I mean, it's not like your father. . . ."

Her voice faded, and Kelsey stared down at her mother's hands twisting together on the tablecloth. She could feel her own chest tightening, and she got up quickly. She couldn't tell Mom about the note — not about *any* of it.

Kelsey jumped as the kitchen door flew open, relaxing again when she saw Justin.

"Oh, so there you are." He looked relieved.

"I'm sorry, Justin. She walked in a few minutes ago. I should have let you know." Mom pulled out a chair and motioned for him to sit, but he shook his head.

"I have to get back. I just wanted to make sure she got home okay. How's Dad?"

"He finally dozed off about half an hour ago. I was hoping he'd sleep a while, but he made me promise to wake him for the search party — "

"Don't do that," Justin shook his head. "I'm going up there now. They're finishing the last stretch this morning, so Skip said he'd close down East Beach and cover for me."

"Let us come," Mom said quickly. "We can do something — "

"No, you need sleep, too," Justin said kindly. "I'd rather you just locked the door and tried to rest."

"But what if someone comes by or tries to call?" Mom argued. "If anyone's heard anything — "

"I doubt anyone would call except maybe the sheriff — and he'll be with us. It's an unlisted number anyway." Justin took a pad off the counter and wrote on it. "Here — just in case you need it. We wouldn't have a phone at all, only Dad needs to keep in touch with his agent. It's the same number for both houses."

"Both?"

"Well, when the phone rings, it rings here and next door, too. That's so one of us will hear it if Dad's locked away with his typewriter going. Except we're usually not around, so Dad always misses his calls."

Kelsey smiled and took the paper he handed her. Justin backed towards the door again and paused.

"The search won't last much longer — maybe you heard. They've covered the whole island, and gone over the cove dozens of times. . . ."

Kelsey felt a knot in her throat. She wanted to say something, but Justin was gone.

"Donna's coming by to take me sightseeing," Kelsey mumbled, but she knew her mother hadn't heard. She slipped quietly outside, turning her face to the sun, taking in deep gulps of fresh, warm air.

"Trying to get a tan on your throat?" Donna ran up laughing and Kelsey swung around, her spirits lifting.

"Boy, am I glad to see you!"

"Need to get away, huh?" Donna nodded understandingly, slipped an arm through Kelsey's, and began to steer her toward the beach. "I saw Justin headed the other way. Things don't look good, do they?"

Kelsey shook her head. "Justin's with the search party. He doesn't think they'll be looking much longer."

"It's such a rotten shame. And Justin is such

a sweetheart, I can't stand to see him sad like this."

"Was Beth a good friend of yours?"

"Not really; she only came this summer. I never got the impression she was — " Donna cast her a meaningful look — "uh . . . you know . . . too bright?"

"No kidding? She sounded to me like she was really sweet."

"Oh, sweet, yes. Always smiling. Always something nice to say to everyone. Kind of like Justin, really — only, you know, *slow*. Like things took a long time to get through to her. But her brothers were really nice to her."

"Even Neale?"

"Yeah, it's funny, huh? Even Neale. Come to think of it," Donna screwed up her face, puzzling, "I never heard him speak a mean word to her. He was always really patient . . . like maybe he realized she couldn't grasp things as fast as everyone else."

Kelsey felt sad. "She must have been pretty special. . . . No wonder there's such a void in the family."

"She seemed to really like both of them," Donna added, staring into the blue sky as if the past was playing there like an old movie. "But she hung out with Justin more than Neale. All this summer she's been a sort of permanent fixture around him. Like when he was working West Beach, she was never very far from his station."

"Did he mind?"

"Never seemed to — and you know how some guys would handle that! I mean, can you picture Skip putting up with a tagalong little sister?" Donna rolled her eyes. "That's funny, isn't it — they grew up never knowing each other, and when they were finally together, they really seemed to get along."

"Maybe. . . ." Kelsey stopped to shake a rock from her sandal, "if she *was* a little slow, they felt sorry for her."

"Maybe." Donna mulled this over, then added, "That makes it even worse, you know. That's what I keep thinking about. That she was kind of innocent and naive . . . and nobody was there to save her."

Kelsey shut her eyes, a flood of unwanted memories pounding through her brain. *No . . . I will not think of them. . . .*

"Hey, are you okay?" Donna shook her gently by the elbow, and Kelsey forced a smile.

"Yes, something just got in my eye."

"Well, you better watch where you're going — the beach is really busy."

Kelsey couldn't believe the change since her walk that morning. Now the shoreline was absolutely jammed with people.

"Where did they all come from?" she asked, amazed, and Donna giggled.

"End of summerers. Trying to squeeze in all their last flings before school starts. The beach'll be empty again when the boat pulls out this evening."

"What happens then? The beach just closes down?"

"Well, it's never *really* closed, not literally, but it's swim-at-your-own-risk after six. I mean, the lifeguards can't just live there twenty-four hours a day!"

"Don't any of the islanders ever use their own beach?"

"Oh, sure, but not that many." They swerved around a volleyball game. "Everyone's been warned about the risks after dark, and really, there's not many kids on the island anymore. They've all grown up and left. A lot of them go to the mainland to work or they're off on exotic vacations."

"And what about you?"

Donna threw her a mischievous grin. "My folks own the fanciest restaurant on Beverly. And am I a lady of leisure? No way! Unfortunately, my folks also believe in the old-fashioned values of hard work and earning your keep! This just happens to be my day off. Tomorrow Mom and Dad jet off to London, and where will I be? Waitressing and bussing tables."

Kelsey laughed and hurried with Donna through the crowds. They had been going in the opposite direction from Kelsey's route that morning, and this part of the beach was like a whole different world. Instead of quiet cottages on the rise overlooking the sand, there was a hodgepodge of food stands, game booths, souvenir tents, bright blue awnings and striped umbrellas, all jammed together with swimsuited bodies and glistening tans. Floating in the salty air was an overpowering mixture of hot dogs, suntan oil, hamburgers and grilled onions, dried shells and seaweed, and hot, hot sun. Laughter and shouting mingled with the rush and break of the waves, blaring radios, the happy screams of swimmers, and through it all came the hollow boom of a voice: "You're out too far! Get closer to shore!"

"Look, there's Skip!" Donna tugged at Kelsey's sleeve, and they stopped beside his tower. "Hey, lifeguard! How's the weather up there?"

"Hey, ladies!" Skip grinned down at them, perfect white teeth flashing in his perfectly tanned face. "Just the usual routine. Let's see . . . oh, I'd say I've saved about two hundred lives in the last hour."

"And broken how many hearts?" Donna flung back.

"You cut me to the quick," Skip tried to look wounded. "Can I help it if they all lust after me? Can I even blame them?"

"Dreamer." Donna aimed a punch, but he dodged.

"And where are you two headed?"

"Thought I'd take her on a tour of the island."

"How grand. That should take all of ten fascinating minutes." He bent over and winked at Kelsey. "You understand, of course, that seeing me was the highlight of the tour. Everything from now on is simply — "

"Garbage," Donna finished smugly. "Don't pay any attention to him — he's a perfect example of what too much sun can do to the brain."

"Is that any way to talk to someone who might one day save your — " Skip broke off, and gave a sharp blast on his whistle. "I said come back!"

"They really respect you, Skip," Donna said, straightfaced. "I'm very impressed." She started to pull Kelsey away, but Skip aimed his megaphone down over their heads.

"Now hear this! Are you coming over tonight?"

"Why would we want to do that?" Donna clamped her hands over her ears, and Skip grinned.

"Because the servants are away, and I want to play. Come on, be a sport. We need some bright moments in our lives. Happiness. Joy. Laughter."

"Sounds pretty boring," Donna faked a huge yawn.

"You'll have me all to yourself," Skip reminded her. "Without all these jealous females around."

Donna tried to hide it, but Kelsey saw the quick flush on her cheeks. "Skip, you really are too much. And why would I ever want you to myself — you know I don't like used merchandise."

"But I'm like fine leather," he deadpanned. "The more I'm handled, the better I get."

"The more stuck on yourself you get," Donna retorted.

"Donna, Donna," Skip said, his tone patronizing. "Now you know you don't mean that. You know how boring tonight will be anyway, all alone in your house with nothing to do."

"So what?"

"So I think you'll come." Skip looked as if he had won a secret battle. "And anyway, you didn't let me finish. I want to get Justin over there. Get his mind off all this horror-movie stuff."

"Oh, Skip," Donna looked uncertain. "I mean, I think it's really nice of you trying to cheer him up, but do you really think he'll feel like coming? And what about Neale?"

Skip heaved a martyred sigh. "I'll even ask Neale. Out of the goodness of my heart." He stared down at them for a moment, his expression turning serious. "I'm worried about Justin, Donna. He just won't let himself believe that she's gone."

"And what do *you* think?" Kelsey spoke for the first time, and they both looked at her as if they'd forgotten she was there.

Skip sighed again and balanced the megaphone on one knee. "I think she fell and drowned. I think she was wandering around the cove where she shouldn't have been, and she slipped, and the tide came in. I don't want to be a pessimist or anything, but it's happened before, people taking chances on the beach after dark. We've just been lucky and found them, that's all."

Kelsey looked startled, staring at Skip while Donna tried to pull her away.

"Come on, Kelsey, miles to go before we eat." Her tone was light, but Kelsey didn't miss its undercurrent of concern.

"So I'll see you later, right?" Skip stretched, trying to catch Donna's parting remark as the girls took off through the crowds.

"If you're lucky!" Donna smiled companionably at Kelsey and once again linked arms with her. "He never changes. Impossible since the day he was born. Oh, well, I'm stupid for being so determined, I guess."

"Did you go away to school, too?"

Donna shook her hair back from her eyes. "No such luck. I go to school on the mainland. Skip went there, too, till he had to go away."

Kelsey looked up. *"Had* to?"

"Well, he's hardly turned out to be the model son," Donna chuckled. "His father finally got tired of bailing him out of trouble and thought boarding school would help straighten him out. It didn't, of course, he kept flunking out. But when you're as rich as Skip, people can be persuaded to make exceptions. Mr. Rochford paid this last school a bundle to keep him, just so Skip could graduate."

"How on earth do you know that?"

"Skip told me. But just between you and me, I think he was actually glad to stay at this school 'cause Justin was there."

They slowed down, the crowds thinning out at last, and Kelsey cast Donna a sidelong glance.

"So what happens now — now that Skip's graduated?"

Donna scuffed her shoes through the sand, laughing. "If you're referring to the ongoing saga of Skip and Donna, your guess is as good as mine. Oh, who am I kidding? Of course I'd love for him to come to his senses and realize just how right for him I am. Goodness, we know each other too well — no one else could put up with us!"

"What . . . about Justin?" Kelsey tried to sound casual, but Donna looked at her knowingly. "I mean . . . is he . . . involved with anyone?"

Donna smiled. "Justin's too shy to get involved with anyone. Of course," she added slyly, "there's always a first time." She gave Kelsey's arm a hard yank and raced ahead to where a yellow shuttle bus was just loading passengers. "Come on! This is where we get on!"

For the next few hours Donna gave Kelsey such an insider's view of the island that she fell totally in love with it. It wasn't just the beach and the village and the festive atmosphere that she found so fascinating — it was the friendly attitude everyone seemed to have. Donna made sure Kelsey visited every store, and afterwards they stopped in at Donna's restaurant and got ice cream to eat on their way back to the beach. As they walked, Donna recalled hilarious moments from her and Skip's childhoods, making Kelsey laugh till she hurt. For the first time, she felt glad to be there, but as they came out through some trees onto a rocky embankment, she saw the cliffs towering close by, and her mood changed abruptly. Suddenly it didn't seem right, she and Donna having such a wonderful time, while somewhere . . . forgotten . . . Beth was —

"What did Skip mean back there?" Kelsey interrupted, and Donna gave her a strange look.

"About what?"

"About people taking chances on the beach after dark, and your being lucky and finding them."

"Oh. That." Donna sighed and climbed over the rocks, obviously following some invisible path that she had taken many times before. "It happens sometimes, even when people are warned. It's like I told you, the guys just can't be on duty all the time. People think they're safe 'cause they're only going in for a minute, just to wade or take a quick dip. . . ."

In spite of the hot sun, Kelsey shivered. "And they —"

"Drown," Donna finished. "The tides are so strong . . . so different all around the island. People just get pulled out before they know it — and there's no one around to help."

Kelsey reached out to steady herself, but Donna was a few paces ahead and didn't see.

"We've had two drownings already this summer. It's not something we publicize — I mean, the last thing we want is for people to be afraid of this place."

"That's . . . horrible," Kelsey murmured. She felt weak, and Donna was getting farther away.

"But like I said, it's lucky they were found. They were both girls about our age — vacationing on the island. I'm glad *I* didn't find them; I think I'd go nuts."

Kelsey took a deep breath, a hesitant step. The rocks were hard to climb, but Donna didn't seem to be having any trouble. "Who *did* find them?"

"Oh, you wouldn't know him," Donna's voice was getting farther and farther away. "His name is Isaac. He's an old fisherman who hangs around the island — really creepy-looking — with an eye patch."

Kelsey stumbled, caught herself, trudged on. "I . . . I do know him. . . ." She wasn't sure if she had spoken aloud or only inside her head, but Donna was calling back.

"There's a really neat view from up here, if I don't have a heart attack first. You can see all the cliffs and both beaches, and Skip's house is just over there — there's a road, but it's usually locked up."

"Road? Donna, are we going to the lighthouse?" Kelsey stopped, but Donna continued to climb.

"Sure! Don't you want to see it?"

"I thought we weren't supposed to — "

"We're not." Donna grinned sheepishly back over her shoulder. "But I love it up here, it's so private and the view is the best. Come on!"

Sighing, Kelsey started after her again, already feeling little ripples of apprehension through her body. She didn't want to run into Isaac again . . . *or* Neale. . . .

"Here we are! Up you go!" Donna gave her a boost, and Kelsey stumbled onto solid ground at last, gasping for breath. "It's a shortcut," Donna said apologetically, putting her arm around Kelsey, steering her forward. "I should have put you in training first — sorry." She didn't seem to notice how Kelsey clung to her as they went closer to the lighthouse. "It's something, huh?" Donna tilted her head, gazing up at the imposing structure. "It was built in 1824. The last lighthouse keeper lived here for over forty years."

Kelsey raised her eyes reluctantly, her fingers clamping onto Donna's arm. Again it was there — *again* — that feeling of being watched. . . .

"They just let it go," Donna said sadly. "After all its years of warning people away from the rocks . . . of course it didn't always help. Lots of ships went down in the cove. Lots of folks still think the lighthouse is haunted . . . that all the souls of the drowned walk in the tower . . . and cry . . . and try to lure new souls to their deaths. . . ."

Kelsey squeezed her eyes shut, trying to force the fear away . . . the cry of the wind . . . the unseen eyes that watched . . . watched. . . .

"Maybe it was them," Donna whispered, "Maybe Beth heard them calling her and —"

"Come on," Kelsey said firmly. She fought down mounting terror and pulled Donna along behind her, hurrying, not really seeing clearly, tugging her back down the embankment as she tried to keep her balance. She heard Donna stumbling along behind her, the wail of the wind, her own heart pounding — and she saw the rocks, weaving unsteadily beneath her feet — but not the thing — she didn't see the awful thing sticking out of the grass, clawing at the air as if it were still alive, clawing at her ankle like a last hope —

She didn't see the thing until she fell, and Donna fell beside her, until she heard Donna scream, and she rolled over, panicky, and reached out to grab Donna's hand.

Only it wasn't Donna's hand she grabbed.

And it wasn't Donna's eyes staring back at her, empty and glazed with horror.

Chapter 7

Kelsey didn't remember getting back down the cliff. It was as if some automatic pilot had taken over and flung them both onto the beach and set their legs in motion. She was vaguely aware of running, of Donna's shout, of people looking at them as if they'd lost their minds, but it wasn't until she heard a horn honking that she came fully to her senses.

"Skip! Skip! Oh, thank God — *Skip!*" It was Donna's shrill voice that shattered the last of Kelsey's stupor, and she saw the jeep slamming to a halt on the sand, and Donna throwing herself on Skip and crowds gathering to listen as Donna babbled. "Skip — up there — you've got to come — Skip — "

He was half out of the jeep with his arms on her shoulders. "Donna, snap out of it. Stop it now, tell me what's wrong — "

"Oh, Skip — up there — "

"*Where?*"

"There — there — " Donna made a blubbering sound, and Skip shoved her into the jeep.

The crowd was growing, people attracted by the shouts, some straining to look up the beach, others starting to walk in that direction.

"Come on, Kelsey, get in."

They took off in a spray of sand, and Kelsey turned her face into the wind, glad for the stinging shock against her cheeks. Donna was still jabbering in the front beside Skip, and from time to time he reached over and patted her, nodding, his face anxious but baffled. As the curious dwindled away behind them, Kelsey could see the cliffs getting closer, and she pressed her fists into her stomach, trying to stop the awful dread.

They jolted to a stop beside the locked gate, and Skip jumped out. "Okay. Where?"

"Up there. On the other side. It was in some weeds." Donna shuddered as Kelsey got out and raised her eyes slowly to the lighthouse. "Shouldn't you call for help?"

"Not till I'm sure I really need it." Skip pulled at the chain around his neck, his expression annoyed. "Terrific — I've lost my key again."

"You guys are *always* losing your keys!" Donna's voice rose. "Skip, *hurry!*"

"No, wait — here it is — " Skip took a blue key from his pocket, fiddled with the lock, and unwound the chain. Then he put his hands on his hips, scanning the face of the rock.

"You don't believe me," Donna said, hurt.

"I didn't say that at all. All I said was — "

"Maybe you should at least call Neale," Donna insisted. "Call *someone*, Skip, *please!*"

"Neale's with his dad on the search party, and Justin's due back any second," Skip mumbled, eyes still studying the rocks above. "And what were you two doing up there anyway? You know better, Donna; you know how dangerous that place is."

"Don't lecture me, Skip!" Donna shouted. He whipped around, and her face was pale and pleading. "Skip, there's really somebody up there — you've got to help her — you've got — "

"You can't help her. I think she's dead." Kelsey bit her lower lip and saw the others staring at her.

Skip let out a low whistle. "Are you sure?"

"Maybe just unconscious — " Donna began, but Kelsey shook her head and walked to the gate.

"No, her eyes were . . . empty. She was dead."

"You . . . you mean you really found a *body* up there?" Skip was staring at them in total astonishment, and they nodded in unison. "Was it Beth?" Skip asked at last.

The girls exchanged desperate looks, then Donna shut her eyes, swallowing hard. "I don't know — it happened so fast — "

"You don't know? What do you mean you don't know — "

"We didn't really see her face!"Donna broke in, panicky. "We just tripped over her — Skip — *get up there!*"

"Okay, okay, just don't get hysterical on me. You wait here."

"No, we — "

"Wait here, Donna, I mean it!"

They watched helplessly as Skip disappeared up the hill. Kelsey wasn't sure just how far down the cliff she and Donna had gone, how long it would take before Skip finally found that awful thing sprawled in the weeds. She could feel her pulse hammering, and when she looked over at Donna, her friend looked back miserably at her.

"What's taking him so long?" Donna groaned. "I thought he'd be hollering by now."

"Maybe he's in shock," Kelsey murmured.

"Or throwing up. That's what I feel like doing, just throwing up." Donna covered her face with her hands, her voice shaking. "Oh, God, Kelsey . . . if it was Beth . . . I swear I really didn't see her face . . . if it is . . . if it — "

"Come on, I'm going for help — no, wait, look, there he is — " As they hurried over to meet him, Kelsey tried to get a glimpse of his face, steeling herself for the worst. But it wasn't grief distorting his face. It was anger.

"I guess you think you're pretty damn cute, huh, you two?" He nodded at them, his lips pressed into a sneer. "Pretty funny stuff, calling me away from the beach like that. What is this, Scare the Lifeguard Day?"

Donna looked flabbergasted. "Skip, what are you *talking* about?"

"Oh, come off it, Donna — okay, so I fell for your stupid joke. Dumb me, ha, ha. You just better hope nobody drowned back there while you've had me on this wild goose chase." Skip shook his head and slammed the gate back into place. "Now get out of here. You can walk back."

"Skip — "

"Hey, wait a minute!" Kelsey ran up, catching his arm, her eyes wide with disbelief. "This *isn't* a joke! Believe me, there's nothing funny about it — there's a girl lying up there, and she was *dead!* Didn't you *see* her?"

"No. And you didn't, either."

"Well, then, you must have looked in the wrong place," Donna was babbling again, grabbing Skip's shoulders, shaking him. "You must have stepped right over her . . . or maybe . . . she rolled down the hill! You shook the ground, and she rolled right down — "

"Rolled right — " Skip rolled his eyes and pushed Donna firmly away. "Donna, you are a typical, illogical, emotional female. Rolled down the hill!" he snorted and climbed back into the jeep. "There is *nobody* up there! Dead or alive! If you don't believe me, go see for yourself."

"No!" Donna looked stricken at the prospect of meeting up with a corpse for the second time, but then she saw the look on his face. "All right, we *will* go back! We'll *show* you!"

"You will *not*. You're not supposed to go up there and you know it. If you go back, I'll have you arrested for trespassing."

"Then come with us. I dare you!"

"Oh. Great, Donna. Terrific. You really *do* want me to lose my job. No way. I've listened to you enough for one day." Skip gunned the motor and the jeep made a sharp half turn.

"You're crazy, Donna. A crazy, lamebrain female if there ever was one."

"But I saw her, too!" Kelsey's voice rang out, firm and clear over Donna's protests, and Skip hesitated. "She was up there, and I fell over her, and her face was only *this far* from mine! I saw her! We both couldn't have made her up!"

Skip pondered this, his green eyes lazily playing over her face, then finally he chuckled. "Okay, I'll give you this one, you guys are pretty convincing. But you better watch out — I'll get you back one way or another."

"Jerk!" Donna shouted as the jeep sped off down the beach. "Didn't I tell you he could be a real jerk? *And* a chauvinist? Sometimes he makes me so *mad!* Kelsey, where are you going?"

But Kelsey was already climbing up over the gate and didn't stop to answer. By the time she reached the top of the cliff she was sweaty and out of breath, but she forced herself down the other side and began to search. Within seconds Donna ran up, gasping, behind her.

"Kelsey — "

"It's not here, Donna. Skip wasn't playing around; it's not here anywhere."

"But that's *crazy*, it *must* be! Something like that just couldn't disappear! Let's look for it! Oh, God, what am I saying? I must be out of my mind; I just said let's look for a *dead body!* Oh, Kelsey — "

"It's no use, it just isn't here." Kelsey shook her head angrily and plopped down on the ground. The lighthouse rose above them, watchful and silent, and Kelsey stared at it, thoroughly shaken.

Donna dropped down beside her. "What are we gonna do? Call the sheriff?"

Kelsey ripped a handful of weeds from between the rocks. "And tell him what?"

"You're right. He'd think we're crazy, too. We can't prove a thing. And Sheriff Rickert hates practical jokes — he'd just as soon throw us in jail as look at us." She grew silent for several long minutes, then glanced uncertainly at Kelsey. "We did see it, didn't we? We didn't imagine it?"

"Things like this only happen in movies," Kelsey grumbled, "not in real life. Oh, I wish you'd seen her face!"

"You do? Why? So I could have nightmares till I die?" Donna was instantly contrite. "Sorry. I wouldn't wish this on anybody, especially you. You think it might have been Beth? Can you remember *anything* about her face?"

Again Kelsey saw those wide-open eyes, staring and vacant, filled with fear. "No," she squeezed her own eyes shut, forcing the memory away. "Just her eyes. The rest of her face was hidden in the grass."

"Then we're back to nothing," Donna sighed. She shaded her eyes and stared off toward the ocean. "I guess I can't really blame Skip for being mad. For thinking it was just some kind of sick joke. It *is* pretty hard to believe. I mean, this whole thing with Beth disappearing and all — he's got to be thinking about all that horrible stuff at school. Those Brookfield Murders."

Kelsey, scanning the slant of the cliff as it meandered to the sea, only half heard her. "What?"

"Oh, those coed killings. Don't tell me you never heard about the Brookfield Murders — it was all over the news."

This time Kelsey sat up and leaned forward.

"I do remember something about that. At least I think I do. Some boarding school, wasn't it? But I don't remember all the details."

"Well, that was Skip's school. Brookfield. Named after the town, also Brookfield. Where he and Justin were roommates." Donna wrinkled her nose and tilted her face into the breeze. "Skip said it got really scary around there for a while, cops swarming everywhere you looked. Girls just started disappearing."

"How horrible. Did he know any of them?"

"He dated some of them." She gave a wry smile. "He told me about them, of course. Said they were all really nice girls — not the kind who'd just walk away with anybody or hop in some stranger's car. He was really upset about it when he and Justin were home for spring break. No clues, no leads, nothing. Those girls vanished into thin air, and no one could find them. They *still* haven't found them."

Kelsey felt a shiver work its way up her spine. "And they never had any ideas at all? Not a single suspect?"

"No, and I guess they thought of everything,

too. Even checked out the local mental hospital to make sure none of the patients had escaped. A mental hospital in the same town as the school — I find that extremely appropriate somehow."

Kelsey laughed but it sounded strangely hollow. Her eyes moved again, restlessly, over the rocks, the wind-worn path, the scrawny plants.

"You seem awfully nervous," Donna said uneasily.

"I am."

"Me, too. I'm scaring myself. Let's go."

Donna led the way up again so she was several yards ahead when Kelsey let out a yell.

"Don't do that!" Donna scrambled back, watching dubiously as Kelsey squatted down. "I almost killed myself! What is it? Oh, God, I can't look — "

"Come on, Donna, it's not a body." Kelsey moved her hands in a wide circle along the grass. "But it's *been* here, don't you see? Look at all this grass, all flat like this — *it's been here!* We didn't imagine it, Donna. It was right here in this exact spot!"

Donna stared down at the vague imprint on the ground, her face pale and blank. "Then where is it? If it was here, where did it *go?*"

"I don't know," Kelsey retorted grimly. "But unless it got up all by itself, something — or somebody — had to move it."

They stared at each other in silence, horrible possibilities washing over them in icy waves. At last Donna sank to her knees and clamped cold fingers onto Kelsey's arm.

"What . . . what if it *was* Beth?"

"What if it *wasn't?*"

A mocking wind howled up over the edge of the cliff. Far below, the ocean hurled itself furiously against the jagged rocks.

Kelsey raised her eyes and stared at the lighthouse, its broken shell resolute and guarded.

"Well, whoever it was," Kelsey said softly, "she sure didn't drown way up here."

Chapter 8

The lifeguard leaned his head against the wall, trembling.

It was strange, he thought, how sometimes now he couldn't even remember what he'd done . . . how sometimes in the morning now he'd have to leave the house very early to make sure if he had had some dream or if it had all been real. . . .

This last one had really scared him.

He'd picked her out special — a runaway with no real family who cared about her, no friends, no one to miss her or report her gone — and he'd been so *careful*, so careful to do it right, do it fast. . . .

And they had *found* her — Donna and Kelsey had *found* her, even while he was racing to get back there because he'd finally remembered . . . and they *found* her before he could do anything about it. . . .

He didn't understand how he could have forgotten and left her there.

He had really known then, what it was like to be afraid.

But he wasn't afraid now.

Now he was safe because she was here with him, hidden where no one would ever find any of them again.

The lifeguard wasn't trembling anymore.

He was laughing.

Chapter 9

"I can't believe you're giving up."

"She's gone, Justin. Why can't you accept it?"

Kelsey could hear them arguing even before she got to the door. Sighing, she sat down on the porch step and stared out through the trees, to the empty beach visible through the branches. It had been a long, long day, and she felt drained.

"You're so damn unfeeling. You're just letting her go."

"Look, they've turned the whole island upside down. They've used dogs and nets and boats and helicopters. What do you think, that I'm not *upset?* That I don't *care?* That I don't lay awake nights trying to think of *one* more thing we haven't thought of? You think I don't worry about Dad? I'm more worried than you'll ever know, Justin — than you could ever *dream!* And not just about Beth — "

Kelsey's mind jostled back to the present. The voices inside the house had gotten louder, and she squirmed uncomfortably, feeling like an eavesdropper but not knowing where else to go.

"About what, then? What's going on with you anyway?"

"Look . . . Justin. . . ." Neale's voice grew calmer, struggling for patience. His silhouette glided by the window. "Look . . . I know this is hard . . . the not knowing. And we might never know. I mean . . . we have to be prepared for that."

"Beth was such a good *swimmer*."

"Okay, Justin, Beth was a *great* swimmer! Beth could have been the best swimmer in the *world* — that still doesn't mean she could have saved herself."

"Why not? What are you saying?"

The silence stretched out, endless minutes, but Kelsey could feel the pain, the tension.

"I'm saying," Neale said finally, quietly, "that no one will ever see her alive again."

"And . . . there's nothing else we can do?" Justin faltered.

A pause, then, "Nothing."

"So . . . this is it."

Kelsey leaned over, resting her forehead on her knees. She heard the screen door creak open behind her, heard bare feet, caught the expressionless glance of Neale as he went by without speaking. She watched as he disappeared through the trees, then turned expectantly as Justin came out onto the porch. He stared at her several seconds, then smiled sadly. "You don't have to stay out here. It's your house, too."

"I didn't want to intrude," she said, making room for him on the step beside her.

He sat down and offered her the Pepsi he was holding, taking a sip when she shook her head. "No intrusion. I'm just trying to drown my sorrows." He winced. "Wow . . . poor choice of words." Kelsey smiled, but Justin added, "He's not telling me something."

"Neale?" She looked up, surprised.

Justin nodded, set the can down in the grass. "There's something on his mind he's not saying. Not that we're all that close, as you've probably guessed by now — but I can tell he's keeping something back."

"What do you think it is?"

"I think. . . ." Justin cast her a sidelong glance, "it has something to do with the way Beth died."

Kelsey stared at him, unsure of how much to ask. At last she said, "What could he know about it?"

Justin lowered his eyes, took a deep breath. "He says she's dead. He's sure of it." His eyes raised slowly, blue and clear and plaintive, drawing hers with their desperation. "How can he be so sure? How can he be so *positive* she's dead unless he knows something the rest of us don't know?"

There was something about the way he said it, the way his voice went suddenly hollow — Kelsey felt an unexpected shudder and gazed at him, unsettled. There was *fear* in his voice, she suddenly realized — *fear* — unmistakable and real and cold — and as their eyes held, she heard him speak again, as from a long way off.

"You don't know Neale," he whispered. "Nobody knows Neale . . . *nobody*. . . ."

"Justin!"

Kelsey jumped as Eric came around the corner of the cottage, and Justin got to his feet.

"Over here, Dad — "

"Where's Neale?" Eric looked from one of them to the other.

"On the beach somewhere; I don't know." Justin made a vague gesture as Eric stared.

"Well, go find him, will you? We need to talk, and I want both of you here." Eric hesitated. I'm sorry Kelsey. I'm really sorry you had to be here for all this."

She opened her mouth to reassure him, but Justin took her arm and pulled her to her feet. "It's okay, he can't hear you anyway. Look, why don't you go on in? You'll have the whole place to yourself for a while."

Despite her troubled curiosity over their discussion, she nodded and watched him go off through the trees. A shower and a nap *would* feel wonderful after everything that had happened today — but first she would call Jenny and tell her about Beth's note. She still felt guilty keeping it to herself if it really *did* mean something. But if it *didn't* — if it was only going to cause more worry and heartbreak — *but that body on the cliff . . . we didn't imagine that . . . and all that talk about girls disappearing. . . .*

78

Kelsey went into the kitchen and found the phone. As she waited for the call to go through, her fingers groped through her pocket and closed around the paper Justin had given her that morning with his private number on it. Kelsey counted the rings — four — seven — and was just about to give up when the familiar voice answered.

"Jen! It's me! I —"

"Kelsey!" A shriek, and then static, while Jenny rambled on about things Kelsey couldn't quite hear.

"Jen, be quiet for a minute, will you? I have something important to tell you —"

"A matter of life and death?"

Kelsey's stomach fluttered. "Could be. Look, Jen —"

"Kelsey, my dad's having a fit out there — we're just leaving for the cabin and —"

"You've got to listen to me! There's this note —"

"Kelsey, I can hardly hear you! What are you on, a twelve-party line? There's this echo —"

"No, it's a private number — Jen —"

"In a minute, Dad! He's really yelling — Kelsey, can I call you when we get back?"

"But that'll be two weeks! Jen, listen to me, *please!*" Kelsey's voice rose. "There's this *note*, the girl I'm staying with thinks someone's going to kill her — *thought* someone was going to kill her, and —"

"You're not making any sense. I — Dad! I said in a minute! It's Kelsey —"

"Only she's missing now — Jen, can you *hear* me? She's missing and she might be dead, and I hid the note in my robe and I don't know if I should *show* it to anyone — "

"What? There's that *echo*, I can hardly hear you, you sound like you're in a tunnel or something — "

"Jen — Jen — *please* — "

"Okay, I'm coming! Kelsey, he's ready to kill me — you know how he gets. Look, I'll call you when I get back."

"But Jen, it's an unlisted number and — *Jen!"* Kelsey wailed as the connection broke, first one click, then another. She stared down at the phone, then slammed it back into place and leaned her forehead against the wall. Now what? Jenny hadn't heard a word she'd said, and she was no better off than she'd been before. Sighing, she dragged herself up the stairs and into the bedroom.

She locked the connecting door between the boys' room and the bathroom and began to undress. The shower felt wonderful, soothing her sore muscles. She hadn't realized just how keyed up she'd been. Rinsing shampoo from her hair, she turned her face up, letting the drops dance across her cheeks, massaging the pain behind her eyelids.

She reached up and shut off the faucet.

And heard something moving in her room.

Naked and dripping, Kelsey stood there, too terrified to move. Silence hung around her, even more horrible than the sound had been. Whatever — *whoever* — it was, *knew* that she had heard. Knew that she was in here right now. Listening. Alone.

Kelsey's heart lodged in her throat, making her feel sick. The silence was crushing her, the awful silence punctuated now by the thud of her racing pulse, her blood pounding ice through her veins.

Kelsey, I think someone is going to kill me. . . .

Her hands were shaking so badly, she could hardly control them. Curling her fingers around the edge of the shower curtain, she tried to pull it back without making any noise. The faucet dripped slowly into the tub, loud plops that echoed like gunshots. There was no sound at all from her bedroom.

Explanations tumbled through her head like leaves in a windstorm. Maybe Neale had come back, looking for Justin, unaware that Justin was out looking for him. Or Justin had knocked and she hadn't heard, and he'd come in trying to find her. Or Mom . . . or Eric . . . or nobody . . . *maybe I imagined it . . . it was the plumbing or something outside or just the house settling and there's absolutely nothing out there. . . .*

Groping, her hands found the towel, and she wrapped it around herself, inching cautiously toward the door. She couldn't hear anything now on the other side — nothing to suggest that anything might be wrong. . . .

Swallowing over the sharp tang of fear, Kelsey shakily called into her bedroom, "Justin, is that you?"

Silence answered her, deep and endless. Slowly . . . slowly . . . she cracked open the door.

The room was just as she'd left it. With a sigh of relief, Kelsey moved out into the middle of the floor, her eyes scanning every surface. Her purse — right there on the desk where she'd left it — her sandals, kicked back under the hem of the bedspread. . . . She smiled to herself and bent down to pick up her robe — it must have slid off the end of the bed when she'd tossed it from the closet. Her knees were still shaking, and she suddenly realized how chilly she felt. She slipped out of the towel and into the robe, easing herself down on the edge of Beth's bed, stretching her legs out in front of her, toes pointed into the rug.

The cold shock of water went through her instantly — the spongy feel of wet fabric against her skin —

She jerked her feet back with a cry and stared in horror at the braided rug between the beds. . . . The rug was soaked with separate little puddles . . . wet spots the size of feet . . . and lying there, coiled like some dead snake, was a slimy tangle of seaweed in a damp smear of sand. . . .

Kelsey jumped up onto the bed, hugging her robe tight around her, her lips forming cries for help that no one could hear. . . .

Someone *had* been in her room.

And maybe . . . even now . . . that someone was still in the house.

Chapter 10

Kelsey hadn't expected it to be so dark. Now as she jerked her clothes on and raced out of the house, she was shocked at the heavy curtain of dusk which greeted her.

Night was rolling in fast with the fog, blurring the outlines of the trees, blotting out the beach but not the persistent sound of the ocean. As Kelsey hurried across the yard she could hear the water off behind her, its roar like mocking laughter — *look at Kelsey run!* — *look at Kelsey run!* She covered her ears and concentrated instead on reaching the pale glow of lights in Eric's kitchen windows.

She started up the back steps and stretched out her arm for the door.

She never saw the hand come out of the darkness. Not until the gnarled old fingers clamped around her wrist and jerked her backward.

"You won't scream, girl, 'cause I been waiting for you. . . ." The voice was liquidy, thick with age and phlegm. "I been waiting for you all this time — "

"Let me go!" Kelsey shoved at him, but only succeeded in losing her balance. She heard him chuckle as she went down.

"I been waiting to tell you a thing or two, so you best listen to old Isaac, you hear me? You best have a care, girl; I see what goes on. And I know things, too, don't think I don't. Just like you know things. You're a smart girl. Like that other one was smart. Only now she's dead." He threw back his head and cackled. From the jaundiced light of the windows, Kelsey could see his yellow teeth and the drool on his bristly chin. "You'll hear it soon . . . the voice of the dead . . . it always comes before the squall. . . ."

"Get away from me or I'll *scream —I mean it!*" She scrambled to her knees, crying out as the porch light suddenly burst on, the door flinging open.

"Have a care!" Isaac hissed, and in the split second it took Kelsey to stand up, he was gone.

"What's going on out here? You all right?"

Kelsey grabbed for the person beside her before she even realized it was Neale. He was squinting off into the dark, searching the shadows.

"That horrible old man — he — "

"Who? Isaac?"

"He's following me!"

Neale gave her a strange look, shaking his head. "He wasn't following you — he was using the phone."

"What?"

"He came to the door a while ago and asked to use our phone — look, I don't have time for your paranoia right now. There's an emergency on the beach and I've gotta get down there." He brushed past her, and Kelsey's voice followed him, fearfully.

"What's happened?"

Neale stopped . . . turned to face her. "A drowning. We . . . someone has to go look at the body. . . ."

Kelsey felt suddenly weak. She sank down onto the steps, her head in her hands, as Neale disappeared through the trees. *Oh, please . . . don't let it be Beth. . . .*

It seemed like he was gone forever. Kelsey sat there, too sick at heart to go inside, knowing everyone would be in there, waiting and afraid. Only when she heard Neale running across the yard again could she finally force herself through the door, unable to take the news alone.

They were all there — Eric and Mom, Justin and Skip — all staring with strangely resolved faces.

"It wasn't her," Neale said. "It was a boating accident — some girl tangled in the anchor line . . . but it wasn't Beth."

Eric covered his face, his voice choked. "No more. I can't take any more of this. . . ."

"Dad," Justin whispered, but Eric looked up, shaking his head.

"No . . . no more. We can't go on like this. We have to stop."

Kelsey stole a look at Justin and looked away again; she couldn't bear the anguish on his face.

"We will . . . of course . . . keep hoping. Always . . . hoping. But it's time to get on with our lives, son." Eric took Justin's hand. "We have to go on. Beth would want us to."

Kelsey saw the room blurring around her. She was aware of movement, chairs scraping the floor, feet shuffling, doors opening and closing — but it wasn't until she felt a hand on her shoulder that she focused in again.

"You're coming with us, aren't you?" Skip asked.

Kelsey twisted in her chair and looked up at him. "Skip," she said slowly, "I think someone was just in my room."

"A lover!" he grinned. "Good for you, Kelsey, smuggling someone in here right under our noses, you little — "

"Skip, I'm serious." Kelsey stared at him, her face drawn. "I couldn't say anything in front of Eric, but — "

"Hey, you're really serious, aren't you?"

"Yes I'm serious. I heard something in my room — and when I came out of the shower, there were footprints on the bedroom rug — "

"What's going on?" Justin came up, leaned on the back of Kelsey's chair as he bent down to listen. "What about your room?"

Before Kelsey could answer, Skip pulled on Justin's arm and headed for the door. "Come on — Kelsey thinks someone was just in her room — "

"What?" Justin looked stunned, glancing back at her as Skip pulled him through the door. Kelsey turned around and saw Neale watching her. A second later he, too, followed the others out the door. Kelsey got up to go with them but as she came out into the yard, she heard Justin's voice, clear and authoritative.

"Kelsey, you stay there. We'll be back."

She shouldn't have said anything — yet, she had heard something — she *couldn't* have imagined it — not after finding the wet footprints on the rug. . . . Kelsey looked around nervously and leaned back against the door. She wished they would hurry.

They were coming back now; she could hear them laughing softly and mumbling to each other as they made their way through the shadows across the yard. No doubt Skip was telling them about her and Donna's grisly discovery that day, and now the boys were finding everything immensely funny. She knew by their faces that they hadn't found anything — but she stood her ground firmly, meeting their looks straight on.

"Kelsey — "

"I know. You didn't find anything."

"Hey, relax, it was probably just that body you and Donna met on the cliff today!" Skip gave her a playful hug, but she stiffened and pulled away, seeing those wide, lifeless eyes again in the grass.

"I don't care what you say, Skip — I heard

something just now. And how do you explain those footprints?"

"What footprints?" Skip chuckled. "I didn't see any — "

"I saw them," Justin broke in, "on the rug, right?" At her grateful nod he smiled. "I saw them. Really. They were there."

"Okay, you saw them. So who put them there?" Skip asked.

"She probably did it herself," Neale said matter-of-factly, shouldering past Kelsey into the kitchen. "She probably just tracked the water in from the beach — "

"You're crazy," Kelsey shot back, and he whirled on her with a look that stopped her cold. "If I tracked the water in, then why wasn't there any in the hall outside my door or on the stairs?"

"There *was* water in the hall and on the stairs," Skip said, deadpan. "You tracked in the whole damn ocean!"

"You're lying," Kelsey whispered, and her eyes fell on Justin, wide, pleading.

"Skip," Justin sighed, and then to Kelsey, "He's lying. But there were footprints from the tub across the floor and onto the rug. You . . . probably did it coming out of the shower."

She couldn't believe what she was hearing. As she stared at three pairs of expectant eyes, she could feel herself going rigid, could hear her voice going thin.

"I didn't make those footprints on the rug! They were already there when I came out of the bathroom! I hadn't even been on the rug before then!"

Justin looked uncomfortable. He dropped his eyes, his brow creased with an anxious frown, and Skip slapped Kelsey on the back with a loud guffaw.

"You're just like Donna — two crazy females! You really expect us to believe that? Look here, Kelsey, if you didn't do it, then who else *could* have? I mean, who'd be wandering around the island going into girls' bedrooms and making puddles, huh? Was anything missing?"

Kelsey shook her head reluctantly. "Well...."

"Well, was it?"

"Well . . . no."

"Okay. Nothing stolen. Nothing ransacked. Nothing vandalized. No murder weapon on the pillow, no suspicious note slipped under the door — "

Kelsey looked up, shocked at his words, but Skip didn't notice and went on.

"Nobody was in your room, Kelsey. All this disappearing stuff is making you paranoid."

"Justin?" She turned to him, her eyes beseeching, and he reached out and took her arm.

"Kelsey, it could have been a lot of things . . . I believe you heard something, but Skip's right — things like that just don't happen on this island."

"You imagined it," Skip dismissed it with a wave of his hand. "It wasn't real. Maybe it was another of your weird dreams, huh?"

"Maybe it was a ghost," Neale said, glancing

at Justin. "Maybe it was Beth coming back to see who was in her room."

The sudden silence was painful. After several seconds Neale turned and walked toward Skip's car. Skip coughed uneasily. Justin sat down on the step, looking disgusted.

"Don't listen to him, Kelsey. He's just in his usual good humor."

"Come on, I think we all need to get out of here for a while." Skip took Kelsey's elbow, but she shook him off.

"I think I'll stay here, thank you."

"Oh, boy," Skip rolled his eyes, "hurt feelings. Okay, I apologize, does that make you feel any better? I apologize for not believing your weird stories. You've been around Donna for exactly one day and already her wild imagination is rubbing off on you."

Justin got up and went inside. "I'll tell Dad we're going."

"Going where?" Kelsey sounded icy, and Skip put on a downcast face.

"To my house. You remember."

"Skip, I hardly think this is the time for a party — "

"Oh ye of little faith, just trust ole Skip here a minute, okay?" He paused, then leaned into her face, his expression sincere. "Look, Justin's my best friend. I just want to get him away from all this for a while. Nothing wild and crazy — just good friends and some positive environment for a change."

Kelsey regarded him primly, and he gave her a hesitant smile.

"Okay, I'm sorry for what I said. If Justin believes you heard something, that's good enough for me. But what or who, I don't know. Personally, I think everyone's jumpy — seeing spooks in every corner. I know it must be tough for you, being in Beth's room and all — that's why I think it was probably just the wind, and you were so scared coming out of the shower, you didn't even remember tracking the water."

"But the seaweed — how do you explain that?"

"What seaweed?"

"Oh, Skip, don't tell me you didn't see the seaweed — "

"Kelsey, I swear, I don't know anything about any seaweed. Footprints, yes. Water, yes. Seaweed, no."

"But the others must have seen it — didn't they say anything — "

"Look, Kelsey," Skip said, taking a deep breath, letting it out slowly, "all I know is that we got in the house and everyone went off in a different direction to see if anyone was hiding in there. You'll have to ask *them* about your seaweed. When *I* got to your room, I didn't see any seaweed. And I didn't smell any saltwater, either." He reached out, gently squeezed her shoulder. "Now come on and go with us, what do you say? I know it'd make Justin happy if you would."

Kelsey didn't know what to think anymore. What he said made a lot more sense than her own fears. After all, hadn't Donna told her how safe the island was? And why would anyone have just walked into the cottage knowing the boys were probably around somewhere? She *was* tired, and she *was* jumpy — and more than anything she didn't feel like arguing anymore.

"What you're doing for Justin," she said at last, "I think it's nice."

"Of course it's nice, I'm a nice guy." Laughing, he gave her a hug and pulled her to the jeep, taking a flying leap into the front while she hesitated by the door.

"Coming?"

She hadn't heard Justin come up behind her, and now she felt his hands on her shoulders.

"Oh . . . I don't think I should," she turned to smile up at him and felt his chin brush the top of her head.

"Why not?"

"Well," she said awkwardly, "this is for all your friends and everything, and — "

"You're my friend." His smile was gentle, and he tapped one finger on her arm. "Aren't you?"

Their eyes held for a long moment.

Flushing, she looked down and stammered, "Well . . . yes . . . I'm your friend."

"I'm glad."

The horn blared, and Skip shouted, "Hey, you two, climb aboard! Donna's meeting us there with the food, and I'm starved!"

"You're always starved," Justin shook his head and boosted Kelsey into the backseat of the jeep, where she squeezed down uncomfortably beside Neale.

"Okay, everyone, hang on!" Skip called, and the next minute the jeep lurched forward, throwing Kelsey helplessly against her seatmate. Neale shrugged her off as if she didn't exist, and they didn't speak a word to each other the remainder of the ride.

Donna had told her how rich Skip's family was, but Kelsey wasn't half prepared for his house. While the boys went out to the swimming pool, Donna gave her a tour of all three floors.

"Do you think we should be snooping around like this?" Kelsey hesitated on the landing, mesmerized by the chandeliers, the fine art on the walls, the sculpture lining the carpeted hallways. "What will his parents say?"

"Not a thing. His dad's on the mainland tonight. Charity ball. His mother's in Paris with her new boyfriend. And anyway, who's snooping? It's practically my house, too." Donna giggled, and Kelsey followed eagerly at her heels.

When they got to Skip's bedroom, all Kelsey could do was stare. The place looked more like an apartment — a two-room suite with couches and chairs, a categorized wall of records and tapes, an elaborate stereo system, plush carpeting, framed prints, a paneled library and solid oak desk.

"Hang on, I smell the pizza burning — be right back!"

Before Kelsey could reply, Donna vanished downstairs, so Kelsey went on in, her eyes roaming the room in disbelief. Another whole wall was encased in glass and held trophies —

swimming trophies — dozens of them. Kelsey walked over and stared, then turned her attention to still another wall covered with certificates and awards, all neatly framed and bearing Skip's name. Standing on tiptoe, she tried to read the top row when a voice from behind made her whirl.

"It's only me," Skip grinned. "Go right ahead. Far be it from me to interrupt adoration."

Kelsey couldn't help but smile. "It'd take me years to admire everything. I've never seen so much stuff. All for swimming?"

"Yeah." Skip threw himself down across his waterbed. "And a few lifesaving awards for good measure."

"You mean you really have saved somebody?"

"Three somebodies, if you please."

"You're quite the hero."

"Aren't I though?" His grin widened. "You know of some body that needs saving?"

Kelsey tried not to blush and turned back to the trophies. "Your dad must be so proud of you."

There was no answer, and after a few seconds, Kelsey looked back at him, surprised by the scowl on his face.

"Did I say something wrong?"

"Not at all. Let me escort you personally around my humble abode." He jumped up again, his mood changed so abruptly that Kelsey regarded him in amazement. He linked his arm through hers and began walking her around the room. "My kitchen, Madame. Very helpful on the cook's night out. You see here the microwave, the refrigerator tucked discreetly beneath my dining table? Ah, yes, and here we have my wardrobe — " he flung open folding doors to reveal a closet as big as Kelsey's living room at home — "all color coordinated and custom designed, and — as you can see by my current and favorite attire of ragged jeans and torn T-shirt — positively useless. Now! Here we have the bath — sunken tub, separate shower, gold faucets, and — watch your step, my dear — out onto this *very* private deck, a Jacuzzi of my *very* own. Impressed? No? Well, well, come right this way and see my darkroom . . . *and* my personal computer system . . . *and* my larger-than-life viewing screen for TV and VCR . . . *and* — "

"*And* there's not going to be any food left if we don't get downstairs!" Donna's voice came authoritatively from the hall, and Kelsey laughed as Skip looked askance.

"My God, she caught us! Now it's blackmail for sure!" He swung an arm around each of them while Donna tried to look disapproving. "All right, ladies, to the pool it is!"

Kelsey stood for a moment on the wide patio, surveying the gigantic swimming pool banked with flowers and ferns, the wooden gazebo, the lattice-covered porch with its bar and stereo and barbecue pit large enough to roast a whole cow. She felt like the newest member of a country club.

"Aren't you eating?"

Kelsey looked up as Justin handed her a paper plate of food. She hadn't realized till now how really hungry she was, and she took the plate, smiling.

"Thanks. It looks wonderful."

"And you look tired." He studied her, worry in his blue eyes. "Feel like sitting down?"

"That would be nice."

He led her to a small table and pulled his chair closer to hers.

"I . . . I've been trying to think of how to thank you."

Kelsey's eyes widened. "Thank me for what?"

"For last night. For telling me you were there."

"Justin, I didn't do anything."

A hint of a smile touched his lips. "You cared. Thank you for caring."

She looked down self-consciously, suddenly intent on her pizza. "I just know how it feels to lose someone, that's all."

There was muffled conversation behind them, Skip and Donna arguing beneath the blare of the music.

"I'm sorry," Justin said. "I'm sorry that you've ever had to lose someone." He didn't pry, and Kelsey blinked back unseen tears.

"So what will you do now?"

"Drink till I pass out?" It sounded so out of character coming from him that Kelsey started to laugh.

A shy smile hovered on his lips once more, as if he were secretly pleased. "I like it when you laugh. You should do it more often."

Flustered, Kelsey toyed with her plastic fork, not knowing what to say.

"I know how you feel," Justin went on. "People always feel that way when something bad happens. They want things to be normal again. They want the bad part to be over so they can get back to their nice, safe routines. But they keep thinking about the victim — about how she can't ever be happy again . . . or normal . . . or sometimes — even alive — " His voice dropped. "And then they feel guilty wanting to get on with their lives." He sighed and pushed back his uneaten food. "Right now all I want to do is be here. Be anywhere. Anywhere but home. Thinking of anything but Beth."

Kelsey nodded but didn't trust her voice to speak.

"I think Neale's right," Justin reflected. "The not knowing, that's the worst. 'Cause then, every day of your life you think maybe today you'll hear something. Maybe today she'll turn up."

"But you can't do that," Kelsey said, surprising even herself. "You can't live your life for something that might never happen. 'Cause then one day your *own* life is over, and all you've done is live for someone else."

Justin watched her, his face thoughtful. There was a light in his eyes, soft, like the sound of his voice, and his sweet, sad smile.

"Feel like taking a walk?"

"All right."

He took her arm, guiding her to a tall gate in a wall at the back of the yard.

"Where are we going?"

"The beach is right out here." He was looking back over his shoulder and didn't notice the way she suddenly tensed. "They're still arguing. They won't even miss us."

"What about Neale?"

"I don't see him. Their fighting probably drove him away. It's what they do best together, fighting."

"She really likes him, you know."

"I know." He held the gate and she went ahead of him, stopping almost at once, unprepared for the sudden surge of darkness.

"It's okay," Justin said softly. "The moon's just behind a cloud. You'll be able to see the whole beach in a second." He reached for her hand, and she held onto him gratefully as he led the way across the sand. The wind was balmy and slow, sighing in over the black eternity of ocean, and the sky sputtered for just an instant, then slowly flooded with light.

Even to Kelsey it was beautiful. As the moon shone down between trails of clouds, the beach shimmered around them — the sand, the rocks, glowing like burnished silver. Far beneath a sprinkling of stars the shoreline gleamed wetly as water tumbled in and out, burbling like a sleepy child at play. Kelsey watched it all, felt its power and beauty and wished, *wished,* that she could love it . . . that the fears would never come to her again.

"Well, what do you think?" Justin asked softly, squeezing her fingers.

Without hesitation Kelsey said, "I think it's

wonderful. And terrifying. I always used to want to live on the beach."

His glance was quizzical. "And now?"

"No," she said quietly, and they kept walking, side by side.

After a while Justin gave her hand a little shake. "Well, this is how the other half lives."

"The other half, meaning you?" she teased, and was rewarded by another almost-smile.

"I was talking about Skip," Justin corrected her. "And all these other mansions we're walking by."

"Are we trespassing?"

"The beach *is* private, but technically we're Skip's guests. And don't forget, I *am* the lifeguard." His tone had taken on a new relaxed sound that Kelsey liked, and she smiled up at him.

"And do you enjoy it? Being a lifeguard?"

He shrugged. "It's a job. I get to meet lots of people — "

"Girls."

"Yeah, okay, girls." His smile was almost embarrassed. "It's certainly not as glamorous as the movies make it. I don't go around rescuing damsels in distress very often, and yes, I *have* gotten sunburn, and no, most of the time people *don't* pay attention when I yell at them, so I have to go out and chase them back in."

"Which beach is your favorite?"

"This one. It's a lot calmer. Not so many accidents waiting to happen. You feel like a swim?"

Without even thinking, Kelsey stopped, jerking her hand free from his. "I . . . no. Not tonight."

"It's really warm," Justin assured her. Going to the water's edge he filled his hands from a burst of spray and let the water trickle onto the sand at his feet.

"I don't have a suit."

"I'm sure there's one back at the house you can use. I'll just go back and — "

"No!" Kelsey tried to control the anxiety in her voice. "No, I mean I don't want to go *swimming*. I hate it." She ducked her head, hoping he hadn't seen the panic on her face, and was disconcerted at the feel of his hand beneath her chin, his fingers tilting her face upward toward his.

"Kelsey, I'm sorry. I didn't mean to upset you. You don't have to swim. You don't have to do anything you don't want to do."

She struggled to tear her eyes away, so conscious now of his touch upon her skin, the way he was looking at her, all kindness and concern.

"It's not that," she whispered.

"It must be something. You seem pretty upset."

She hadn't realized she was trembling. Now she mustered all her resolve and backed away, forcing a smile.

"I just don't like the water, you know? Like some people never like spinach or going to the dentist or taking their finals?"

"Did something happen when you were little to make you so afraid?" he asked gently.

Two years ago . . . two endless years of remembering. . . . "I haven't always been afraid."

"But you're afraid now."

Kelsey nodded. "But you should go in and swim if you want to. I'll stay here and watch."

"No. Let's go back to the house."

"No, really!" Kelsey's voice rose. "I'll feel like I've spoiled it for you —"

"Kelsey, don't be silly. I can swim anytime I want to."

"Please, Justin! I don't want to be afraid of it!"

She didn't know why she said it; the words had tumbled out as if eager to be free of her once and for all. Justin gave her a strange look, and then slowly began to pull his sweatshirt up over his head.

"All right. I'll go in. You'll see it's really nice. Warm and soothing. Like a massage after a hard day's work."

She stood there, watching him, as he kicked his jeans away and straightened the band of his swim trunks.

"I'll go in," he said again, "and then you can come closer."

"No . . . I'll sit here."

"Just to the edge. Right here. See? The water doesn't even come up this far." Justin backed away from her, very slowly, his eyes never leaving her face. She took one cautious step, balked, and crossed her arms tightly over her chest, shaking her head at him.

"No — I don't want to get my clothes all

wet — I'll just watch you. I can see fine from — "

"You've got shorts on, and that practically counts as a bathing suit. Just think of it as going wading," Justin chuckled. "In a giant bathtub." He was in the water now, surf bubbling gently up over his calves, and he reached out his hand to her. "Come on. Hold onto me."

"I can't."

"Yes, you can. I won't let go of you. We'll just stand here and give you time to get used to it."

Kelsey felt her feet moving, carrying her forward as if they belonged to someone else. There was a roaring in her head that hadn't been there a moment ago.

"A little more," Justin urged. "That's right — "

She felt the sand dissolve beneath her feet, like the earth melting away, and the steady warmth of Justin's fingers, tightening over her own.

"See? Nothing to it." His eyes were so blue, even in the moonlight she could see them, and they were gentle, gazing at her encouragingly. In spite of herself she gave a nervous laugh, and he laughed with her, drawing her closer, so that once more she was tucked protectively beneath his chin. "Okay?" he whispered.

She drew a ragged breath, felt his arms go around her as one wave, larger than the others, dashed recklessly against their legs, throwing her against his chest.

She nodded, not quite trusting herself to

speak. The dread was still there, the awful feeling that something bad would happen if she challenged her fears too far. But with the dread there was also something else — a racing in her heart, a warmth spreading through her at the feel of Justin's bare skin against her cheek.

"I know what it's like to be afraid," Justin whispered.

She looked up at him, so sorry for all he'd been through, and he read the sympathy in her eyes.

"It's all right." His lips moved against her hair, her forehead, closing her eyes, hesitant upon her cheek. Kelsey didn't realize she'd been holding her breath until she felt him pull back from her, heard him laugh, almost guiltily. "Well, I guess this isn't much of a swimming lesson."

Now it was her turn to feel shy. She lowered her eyes and laughed with him nervously, staring at his strong, slender hands that still held her. "Maybe we should get back," she said, hoping the quiver in her voice wasn't giving her away. She didn't want to go back. She wished they could just stand here this way forever, with Justin keeping all the terrible fears at bay.

He squeezed her arms. "Not until I show you how much you're missing. Come on. That's right. Another two steps. Just follow me — "

"Justin — " Her fingers clamped down on his arms as he guided her out into the water, but his voice was soft, soothing her, his lips upon her ear —

"Ssh, now, just hold onto me — "

"Justin — no — "

"I've got you, Kelsey. I'm not going to let go of you — "

The world was disappearing beneath her feet; she had no choice but to hang onto him as he waded farther out into the water. She felt the undercurrents bubbling around her ankles and instinctively kicked away from them, thrusting herself out into the deeper waves and into Justin's arms.

"See?" Justin's face was so close, his smile growing. "See? You're doing it. I knew you could."

And she *was* swimming, the old muscles taking over as if they'd never forgotten how, her body light and buoyant in the protective circle of Justin's arms. She felt a strange thrill — triumph? Apprehension? Relief? She wasn't sure what it was, only that Justin's lips closed over hers, and the salt and the warmth of him and the gentle waves lapping their bodies together as she held onto him, tighter . . . tighter. . . .

She never saw the huge wave rumbling toward them.

Or the one that came after, tearing them apart —

What she did see was an explosion of darkness, and stars cartwheeling across the sky, and a moon hung upside down as the ocean somersaulted her onto the shore.

Chapter 11

"Justin!"

Coughing, Kelsey scrambled up out of the
wet sand, slipping, falling, her eyes desperate
upon the slow, pulsing surface of the water.
Nowhere was it broken by a familiar silhouette
— no sign of a body swimming toward shore,
no cries for help, no head bobbing suddenly to
the surface. . . .

There was just the empty beach . . . the
ocean with its secrets . . . and Kelsey.

"*Justin!*" she screamed again. Panic-stricken
she ran into the water, gasping as it crept up
her thighs. It was *her* the ocean had wanted,
not Justin, but she had tempted it too far,
and now she would be punished for her daring.
She had cheated it once . . . and it would keep
trying and trying until — "Justin! Where are
you? Answer me!"

In utter helplessness she stood there, fists to
her mouth, frenzy welling up in her in cold,
choking waves.

And that's when she felt something bump against her leg.

At first, in the strange, slow motions that only fear can produce, she looked down in a kind of detachment, surprised that she wasn't alone as she had thought, half expecting to see Justin's body paddling furiously toward shore.

Only it wasn't Justin's body.

There was nothing there.

And again she felt the curious surprise, something almost like wonder, propelling her like a doll, making her look all around for whatever had made her stumble.

And then it made her stumble again.

And the water parted in a long, wide ripple, moving slowly, deliberately, away from her. . . .

She watched it, hypnotized, the ocean splitting beneath the moon . . . and Neale's voice, grim and prophetic, driving relentlessly through the fog of terror and into her brain. "*. . . don't need deep water . . . three feet will do. . . .*"

And as she gazed at the smooth, clean break in the water, she saw it swing back in a gentle arc . . . saw it coming straight for her . . . saw something rise, bladelike, beneath the moon. . . .

Sheer terror flung her onto the beach once more — screams echoing over and over in her head, the sand crumbling beneath her feet, scraping her hands and face as she fell — ran — fell — ran — the whole beach a macabre funhouse where she raced for her life but never got anywhere. Lights swam by in a dizzying stream — *Where is everybody? Can't they hear? Don't they care?* — and she ran, crying Justin's name that nobody heard —

She tripped over some driftwood and sprawled flat, blood gushing from her nose, and as she stumbled to her feet, arms grabbed her from behind, nearly sending her into hysterics.

"What is it? Kelsey! Stop it!"

She fought the hands that tried to steady her, swinging out at the wet body wrestling to hold her still.

"Let me go! Oh, God — "

"What the hell's the matter with you?"

She saw Neale's black eyes, his scowl; she tried to twist free, but his grip was too strong.

"Justin — " she babbled — "back there — "

"Where?" He shook her. "What about Justin?"

"He disappeared," she sobbed. "I saw a shark — "

Even in the shadows Neale's tan went white. He shoved her roughly in front of him.

"Show me where — "

"You've got to get help — "

"Show me — *now!*"

Together they raced back down the beach, Kelsey trying to keep up with Neale's effortless sprint. She felt sick, undigested seawater and absolute terror churning up into her throat. Her muscles shrieked in exhaustion, but when she stumbled, Neale ran on and didn't stop.

"Where?" he called back over his shoulder. "Where were you?"

"I don't know!" Kelsey cried, pitching forward, struggling up again. He was getting farther ahead of her, and her legs were giving out. She could hear him calling Justin's name over and over again.

"What do you mean you don't know?" he yelled angrily.

"I don't know!" Kelsey screamed back at him. "I know we were past the houses and the lights — I don't *know* the beach, Neale — I don't *know!*" She felt herself losing all mental control but she couldn't help it. She ran up just in time to see him dash into the water.

"Justin!" His voice thundered across the waves, came back mockingly on the wind.

"Neale, don't go in there!" Kelsey looked wildly around, searching desperately for some landmark, some sign of where they had been. It all looked the same — black and empty — and dead. She raced up behind Neale and tried to pull him back. "Neale — we've got to get help — "

"Let go — just get back — " He went deeper, leaving her helplessly on shore.

"Neale! Please!"

"Justin!" he shouted again. "Justin!" Looking back, he waved one arm in a direction farther down the beach. "Go to the lifeguard station and use the phone — just take it off the hook —"

But Kelsey was already running. Gasping painfully for breath she pushed herself along the shore, legs pumping, prayers whistling through clenched teeth, eyes fixed ahead, willing herself forward. *Only minutes away . . . only seconds . . . I couldn't help Dad before . . . I couldn't save Dad before . . . but I'll save Justin. . . .*

She hardly noticed the sound at first. A soft, indistinct sputter, like a cough, only liquid. She thought it was her own throat, that she was going to be sick at last — but when she glanced down and saw the long shadow stretched half out of the water, she gave a shriek and fell down on the sand beside it.

"Justin — oh — Justin — are you — ?"

He heaved, ocean water emptying again and again from his lungs, and she held him until his body lay quiet once more. She was vaguely aware that somewhere in between the spasms she shouted for Neale, and that Justin was shaking uncontrollably as she eased him over onto his back.

She wasn't prepared for the terror in his eyes.

"Where is he?" Justin grabbed onto her, trying to pull himself up, to look around at the deserted stretch of sand, and she fought to push him back down.

"Who? Neale? He was going in to look for you and — "

"No!" Justin was squeezing her arm so tightly that she winced. "Where was he when I went in the water — "

Kelsey stared at him as if the water had somehow affected his reasoning. "I don't know, but I've got to go back and get him!" She tried to pry his fingers away, but he only held her tighter. "Justin, he's gone in to look for you!

I saw a *shark* out there — you don't understand — "

"No!" Justin looked up at her, his face pleading, his voice sinking to a whisper — "No . . . *you* don't understand. . . ."

Kelsey felt a chill ripple up her spine. For a long moment she stared into his eyes, so bright with fear, and didn't even realize at first that someone had slipped out of the shadows to join them.

"Are you all right?" Neale's deep voice fell between them, and Kelsey looked up in alarm. Justin was still trembling. She slipped her fingers around his cold ones and squeezed.

"He's freezing," she said. She watched in silence as Neale knelt down to examine him. Justin lay there passively, too weak to even move. *Weak? Or afraid?* The thought hit Kelsey unexpectedly. With a slight shock she studied Justin's face and watched the color drain away. She released his hand and stood up.

"Where are you going?" Neale asked quietly.

"To get help. He needs a doctor."

"No. He's okay." Neale rocked back on his heels, fixing her with a level stare.

"But he's shaking and — "

"I've checked him over. He's fine. We'll let him rest for a while, and then you can help me get him back to the house."

Kelsey frowned, a strange apprehension creeping over her. This was all too much . . . first Beth and now Justin . . . so easily . . . right in front of her eyes . . . and nothing she could do . . . *nothing* . . . just like before . . .

110

*just like the last time . . . only I wouldn't have
let you die, Justin . . . I wouldn't have. . . .*

She choked back a new wave of panic and
looked over at Justin as he shifted uncomfortably on his back. She saw his eyelids close . . .
saw his lips move . . . saw Neale bending closer
to catch the half-murmured words that were so
hard to hear. . . .

But Kelsey heard them.

Staring at Justin's pale, exhausted face,
Kelsey heard them and the fear that filled them.

"Neale . . ." Justin whispered, *"where were
you?"*

Chapter 12

"I don't know what I would have done," Donna said for the fifth time. She poured boiling water over the teabag in Kelsey's cup and stood back to look at her. "Out there all alone in the water like that, and Justin disappearing —"

"Donna, we have to talk," Kelsey pulled the blanket tighter around her shoulders and eyed her friend dismally. "Someone was in my room tonight, only nobody believes me."

The teakettle clattered down onto the stove. "Are you kidding?"

Kelsey's serious expression convinced her. "The boys don't believe me — I should never have told them. They think I imagined the whole thing. They think I tracked water across the floor onto the rug, only it wasn't me, and there were footprints."

Donna looked puzzled. "You mean . . . someone was prowling around in your room?"

"I can't prove anything," Kelsey groaned. "It's as bad as what happened today, finding that body that disappeared. *Which,* by the way, Skip told the other guys about. They think it's hysterically funny."

"They would," Donna grumbled. "Now Skip'll tell the sheriff and no one'll believe us. Damn him!" Donna slammed her potholder onto the counter.

"You better take Justin his tea," Kelsey reminded her, and Donna grudgingly took the cup and went out of the room. Kelsey could hear them all in the den — all their easy, comfortable voices weaving in and out through the music on the stereo, as if nothing had happened. Even Justin, who had stretched out on the couch, sounded like his old self. Kelsey was proud of herself, really, for having kept up her controlled façade this long. Neale had been very explicit about not wanting to upset anyone, not wanting to create a scene. She had been calm and steady all the way back from the beach; she had brushed off Skip's and Donna's alarm at their long absence, and she had done her share of reassuring and understating. But now — now in the warmth and brightness and safety of the kitchen, she felt herself slowly crumbling apart.

"Are you warm enough?"

The voice startled her, and she looked up. Neale was leaning in the doorway, all angles and shadows and expressions she couldn't read. She looked away and concentrated on stirring her tea.

"Yes, thanks. I'm fine." *No tears now, Kelsey, not the time, not the place. . . .* She wondered if he noticed how her spoon clattered against her cup, how it wobbled though she tried to hold it still.

"About the shark," Neale said, coming into the room. He paused beside her, and she stiffened. "Are you . . . *sure* . . . you saw it?"

Kelsey's mouth tightened obstinately. "Why? Do you think I hallucinated everything back there? Like the prowler in my room? Like the body Skip thinks Donna and I made up? You think maybe Justin just washed himself up on the beach to scare us all to death?" She was shocked at her own belligerence. She glanced at Neale, but his look was one of cool assessment.

"The shark," he said again, as if her outburst had never come. "Couldn't you have mistaken it for something else?"

"I saw it come up out of the water," she said stubbornly. "It bumped against my legs — " She shuddered at the memory, her cup rattling in its saucer.

"Lots of things could bump you underwater," Neale said, going over to the counter, pouring a mug of strong coffee. He raised it halfway to his mouth, his lips pursed to blow. "Fish . . . driftwood . . . seaweed. . . ."

"I felt it," Kelsey said. "I saw it."

"I'm not saying you didn't feel and see *something*." Neale narrowed his eyes. "But sharkskin feels really different — it's rough like sandpaper and you could have been scraped pretty bad. I'm just saying that things can seem pretty scary out there on the ocean after dark."

Kelsey lapsed into uncooperative silence. She felt like she was going to explode.

"Don't say anything about it," Neale's eyes pinned her over the rim of his upturned cup. "At least not just yet."

"Don't you think people have a right to know if they're about to be eaten alive — "

"Sure I do," he lifted his cup in a mock toast. "And they will. But there's no need for complete panic about this. Just let me notify the right people so they can handle it the best way. Does *that* meet with your approval?"

Kelsey looked daggers at him, gripping the hot cup so tightly that her fingers burned. Neale walked out without a word, brushing Donna aside as he went.

"Well!" Donna looked surprised. "What was that all about?"

"I *hate* his — his — *superior* attitude!" Kelsey sputtered. "And the way he's always *bossing* people around! And he's always showing up where you don't expect him — like a snake under a rock. Donna, where *was* he anyway?"

"When?" Donna groped around in the pantry and pulled out a new tin of coffee.

"Tonight. When Justin and I left."

"I don't know. When you and I came down from Skip's room, I don't think Neale was around then."

"I don't think so, either." Kelsey's face puckered in a deep frown, and Donna glanced at her curiously.

"I didn't even realize you and Justin were

gone. Skip and I were fighting. . . . Then he stormed off somewhere, and I came in here to throw things around." She grinned sheepishly. "And the next thing I knew, Skip was out in the pool again and you and Justin and Neale were coming back." She stopped in the middle of measuring coffee. "Kelsey, what's wrong?"

"Where is he . . . where was he when I went into the water. . . ." Kelsey shook her head slowly, trying to clear it of Justin's words on the beach. . . . "Donna . . . do you think Justin seems . . . well . . . *afraid* of Neale?"

For a moment Donna looked perplexed. "Afraid? Everyone's a *little* afraid of Neale, aren't they?" she said wryly. "Nobody gets along with him — not Skip, not the islanders, not even you!"

"Why not the islanders?"

"Something about him makes people uncomfortable. He isn't one to return friendly gestures, if you know what I mean."

Kelsey gave a curt nod. Her nerves felt stretched to breaking, and a headache was throbbing behind her temples.

"Where are you going? Are you okay?" Donna watched carefully as Kelsey stood up.

"I just need a bathroom. I'll be fine in a minute."

"Go upstairs. It's a lot quieter. Third door on your left. Do you need me?"

"No, thanks. I'm just jumpy."

Donna looked sympathetic. "Okay, but if you're not down in ten minutes I'm coming to check on you."

Kelsey couldn't quite manage a smile. She went unsteadily up the wide, curving staircase and found the bathroom. Locking the door, she sat down on the carpeted floor, her back against the wall, and let a horde of memories trample through her mind. She couldn't forget what had happened tonight — the helpless panic of seeing Justin disappear, of seeing that dark shape cut through the water . . . that pressure of something solid and very real against her legs . . . and then the unbelievable relief of finding Justin alive and unharmed . . . when she thought she'd lost him . . . lost him forever . . . *I can't go through that again . . . I can't. . . .*

"Don't . . . struggle . . . it'll be easier if you don't. . . ."

"Oh, Dad," Kelsey whimpered.

She pressed her palms flat on either side of her head, rocking slowly. *Why did Justin seem so terrified of Neale? And why is Neale being so secretive about what happened?* The questions pounded, making her headache worse by the second. *And where did that body go? And why was I so certain that someone was in my room tonight, waiting while I waited . . . listening while I listened . . . ?*

Stumbling to the window, she thrust it open and pressed her face against the screen. The air was damp and soft, and she breathed it in greedily, letting her eyes roam across the rocky coastline, the deserted beach. . . .

Only it wasn't deserted.

Kelsey felt her body go rigid as one of the rocks seemed to lurch away from the others.

Long and ghostlike, it spilled out across the sand, righted itself, finally staggering out into the moonlight. It took half a second to recognize him then. Isaac.

Totally absorbed, Kelsey watched as he approached the wall separating Skip's backyard from the beach. He looked around furtively, shoulders hunched, before he finally flattened himself against the gate.

Kelsey inhaled sharply. Slowly the gate began to open. Isaac wedged one shoulder in and paused.

"Skip!" Kelsey hit the stairs at a run and burst into the den. "Skip — in back — he's trying to break in — "

"What! Who?" Skip stared at her, not fully comprehending, and Kelsey wondered if he'd been drinking. Justin and Neale were already running out the door to the pool. Donna jumped up and looked at Kelsey, and Skip finally grumbled and followed the other boys outside.

"Are you okay?" Donna grabbed Kelsey by the wrist and they raced out into the yard, just in time to see Justin and Neale run out through the gate.

"I saw him from the window — " She waited breathlessly for the sounds of a struggle. "They should have caught him by now. He was halfway in the gate — "

"Well, there's nobody there now," Skip spread his arms wide, letting them drop again loosely to his sides. "You said 'he' — "

"Yes, it was Isaac."

"Isaac!"

"I'm sure of it. I could see him plain as day."

"What's he hanging around here for?" Donna asked, more annoyed than frightened. "Doesn't he have anything better to do?"

"Oh, he probably heard the music and wanted to join the party." Skip grinned as Justin and Neale came back into the yard. "Any luck?"

"Not a sign of life anywhere." Justin latched the gate and added, "What happened to your security system, anyway?"

"It hinders my comings and goings," Skip said wickedly. "I disconnect it whenever possible."

"Kelsey said it was Isaac," Donna added.

"Isaac? What the hell's he doing here?" Neale muttered. He tossed Kelsey a curious glance as he passed.

"I didn't imagine it," Kelsey said icily.

"Did I say you did?" Neale sounded unconcerned.

"You *implied* it. I saw him from the window upstairs."

"That's all right," Justin stepped in. "We're all a little jumpy. And Isaac's harmless."

"Nobody," Skip lifted his beer can, "is harmless."

"He's right," Neale said, and Skip looked at him in surprise. "How well can you ever really know anyone?" He disappeared into the house, leaving the rest of them in an uneasy huddle.

"I think we should go home," Justin said. He laid one hand gently across Kelsey's back and nodded. "This is enough excitement for one evening. Got your things?"

She couldn't remember where she'd left her purse, and had to go back through the house looking for it. At last she found it in Skip's room on a chair, and was just bending down to get it when she heard someone come in behind her.

"Couldn't stay away, huh." Skip gave her that teasing smile, and she breathed a sigh of relief.

"Skip, you scared me half to death. I was just looking for my purse."

"Oh," he looked disappointed, "I thought maybe you'd come to finish the tour."

"You mean there's more?" she laughed.

"Oh, my *dear*," Skip draped one arm around her neck and guided her clumsily to another door not far from the darkroom. "I am just *full* of surprises, shocks, and thrills — " He pushed the door wide and raised his voice in a falsetto fanfare. "TADA! And here we have *the* eighth wonder of the world — " He swept his arms to encompass the crowded exercise room, and Kelsey burst out laughing as she saw what the "eighth wonder" was — a full-length mirror in which Skip's image grinned back at her.

"Well, aren't I right? Aren't I the next international monument?"

Kelsey shook her head. "You're a wonder, all right." Besides all the gym equipment in the room, the walls were hung with mounted animal heads, obviously very much alive at one time. Stuffed pheasants, frozen in flight; ducks with shiny feathers; a small red fox with beady black eyes. . . . She took a nervous step backward, and then she saw the deer — the delicate face and slender neck of a doe, the eyes wide and soft and trusting, the quintessence of gentleness. Kelsey felt a shiver of revulsion, a wave of sadness — strange . . . the eyes reminded her of Justin. . . .

"Skip," she mumbled, not wanting to stay one more minute in the presence of this horrible display.

"You don't approve," he said blandly, not seeming surprised at all. He lifted a beer can, and his mouth curled up in an apologetic grin. "Well, neither does my dear, sweet mother. That's why I have them all hanging in here away from the general public. Another trophy room of mine, I guess you could say. And here I thought you'd be impressed by my primal hunter's instinct."

"I . . . I just don't see how you could have . . . killed that deer." Kelsey turned to him, disappointed. "They're so sweet and helpless. . . . "

"It's the tracking, really," Skip went on as if he hadn't heard her. "The tracking . . . going after them . . . and the prey . . . unsuspecting. . . . " His voice lowered, eyes fixed on the deer head high on the wall. "So helpless, and you run it down. . . stalk it till it's finally yours." He snickered, and Kelsey felt a chill snake up her arms. "It's the tracking, Kelsey, that's the real fun of it," he whispered. "They don't see you . . . but they know. They know you're there, and they know they're going to die. Sometimes," his eyes fell on hers, "you can even smell their fear, it's so strong."

Kelsey pushed him aside. "Skip, you're drunk. I'm going home."

"And that completes *this* particular tour," Skip announced. "Of course, there *are* more *private, exclusive* tours I'd be more than happy to sign you up for." His eyes twinkled blearily as he looked her up and down, and Kelsey gave him a tight smile.

"What I can't understand," she said, "is how you could ever stand to go away to school and leave all this."

"Why?" Skip feigned alarm, drawing back with a gasp. "Why, indeed!" He fell back on the waterbed, looking peculiarly smug. "Number one — I am a very, *very* unmanageable son, and dear old Dad wants me out of his hair. Number two — am I going too fast for you? — I am the *ultimate* embarrassment to my saintly mother, who doesn't happen to be here now, by the way, because she's having a new affair that no one's supposed to know about, but, of course, everyone does. And number three — the reason that I'm a very, *very* unmanageable son *and* the ultimate embarrassment is because this place is a stinking prison!"

Kelsey hadn't expected this — she stared back at him in silence, trying to make up her mind just how drunk he really was. His face wore that same mocking expression it always wore, but as he looked back at her, his mouth trembled and he gave a forced, weak laugh.

"A prison, in case I didn't make myself clear. A prison of . . ." he frowned, searching for the word, then snapped his fingers, "of privilege!"

Kelsey didn't know what to say. Suddenly she felt like an intruder, who had no right to hear these things.

"You're right, Kelsey," Skip said, very quiet now, "I probably am drunk." He twirled the beer can slowly between his fingers, then shook his head. "No. I'm not drunk. I couldn't do that to Justin, not tonight." He smiled at Kelsey, and she smiled back, believing him. "No, Kelsey, it's a strange, strange world I live in, this land of the rich and greedy. Everyone thinks I have everything."

"And do you?" she asked softly.

"I'm used to getting what I want." His smile twisted, went bitter. "And what I don't get . . . well . . . I just take."

Kelsey felt her smile falter, fade. She looked at him uneasily, then turned as Justin's voice floated up from the stairs.

"Kelsey, we're leaving!"

"Yes, I'm coming!"

Skip raised his beer can in farewell. "To our next meeting?"

"Skip, you either have to drive us home, or we're taking your car!" Justin yelled, and Skip clambered up with a sigh.

"That's what I get for giving the chauffeur the night off. . . . "

Kelsey was glad to rejoin the others, and this time she sat in the backseat beside Justin. The night had turned chilly, and as the jeep sped homeward, she was conscious of Justin's arm protectively around her, his chest and shoulders shielding her from the wind. When they finally reached the cottage, Neale jumped out first, eyeing them coolly as Justin casually withdrew his arm and nudged Kelsey out.

"I'll call you tomorrow," Donna promised. "I know a great place for a picnic — breakfast, okay?"

"Well, some of us have to work for a living," Skip said, ruffling Donna's hair. She ignored him. "See you guys tomorrow — "

There was a chorus of good-byes, and Kelsey followed the boys into the house. Neale went straight upstairs and closed the door. Justin hesitated in the hall outside Kelsey's room, waiting for her to turn on her lamp.

"Justin, are you sure you're all right?" Kelsey asked again. She looked into his eyes, searching for answers.

He nodded. "But what about you?"

"I'm okay. You know you really terrified me tonight — I really thought — "

"Ssh . . . " His finger touched her lips. "Me, too . . . but it's over now. Everything's okay."

"Is it?" She wasn't sure why she said that, wasn't sure if she just imagined a shadow flickering over his face. "Justin, what happened out there? I was standing right next to you — if it was an undertow like Neale said, then why didn't I get washed away, too, and — "

"It wasn't an undertow," Justin said softly.

At first Kelsey thought she'd misunderstood

him. She stared, frowning, letting his words sink in. "What . . . ?"

"I know what Neale said, Kelsey, but he was wrong. I didn't want to scare anybody back there, especially you. But it wasn't an undercurrent or anything like that. It was like — I don't know — " He shook his head slowly, as if trying to recall the exact feelings, the exact fear — "like something alive grabbed me from underwater. Grabbed me and pulled me down." He glanced at her, almost guiltily. "Maybe I imagined it . . . maybe I panicked when I went under . . . it just felt. . . . " His eyes closed for a second, a brief flash of pain creasing his brow.

"Justin," Kelsey whispered. She sounded frightened, and he looked annoyed with himself.

"Listen to me, standing here inventing things to worry about . . . what matters is that we're both okay. Let's not think about it anymore."

"But you could have been — "

"But I wasn't." He smiled down at her, his body relaxing a little. "I guess I owe you another swimming lesson."

"No, I don't think so." His eyes were so blue . . . so clear . . . and she couldn't look away. . . .

"Good-night, then."

"Good-night."

She slipped into her nightgown, pulled on her robe, and perched on the edge of her bed. So much had happened . . . so much that wasn't right. . . . She had to think.

Her eyes lowered, fell again on the rug at her feet. The stains were still there, lopsided rings of faded dampness, but the seaweed was gone. She stared hard at the spot where it had been, seeing it again in her mind, and she knew with fierce certainty that she hadn't imagined it. She got down on the floor, crawled slowly from the rug to the door, eyes narrowed and intense. No footprints here. No water marks, no leftover stains . . . *"when I got to your room I didn't see any seaweed. . . ."* When had the other boys gotten to her room? And where had the seaweed been then?

Kelsey crawled back to the rug and started over again, toward the bathroom door.

What she found there turned her cold.

She hadn't noticed it before — she was positive it hadn't been there or she'd have stepped on it. But now — now it was lying just beneath the bathroom door — as if someone had tried to push it under and it had snagged — almost hidden, but not quite — just that one matted glob that had started to dry and work its way free and now left a little trail across the floor like a strand of damp hair. . . .

With trembling fingers Kelsey reached out . . . horrified . . . touched it. . . .

She jerked her hand back, but the seaweed clung, and she cried out as she tried to fling it off, to unpeel it like dead skin. . . .

The awful thing sailed across the floor, landing with a thud.

Kelsey's hands flew to her heart, her throat, fluttered to her mouth and finally to her pocket, where they froze as a look of disbelief contorted her face. For suddenly in the far reaches of her mind, she heard Jenny's voice again over the phone, struggling to get through — *"there's that echo — Kelsey, you sound like you're in a tunnel or something — that echo!"* — and she'd been *trying*, trying so *hard*, to tell Jenny about the note, only Jenny hadn't heard a word she'd said. . . .

But somebody had.

Because when she had hung up the phone, there had been *two* clicks, not one. . . .

Somebody had listened in and heard everything.

And now the note was gone.

Chapter 13

The sky was just glowing pink when Kelsey slipped out of the cottage. She paused on the steps and slid her arms into her purple windbreaker. She hadn't heard the footsteps behind her. Now as that shadow took form beside the house, she stifled a scream.

"You're up early," Neale said. She could feel the intensity of his stare, even though his eyes were part of the morning darkness, and she tried to stare back, undaunted.

"So are you."

"I always am." He moved off and climbed into his jeep. "You need a lift somewhere?" he asked without looking up.

"No . . . I was just going for a walk."

"Suit yourself." The jeep's engine grudgingly came to life. Kelsey watched as Neale aimed it for the break in the trees.

"Neale!" she called. "Wait!" She suddenly found herself clutching the door handle and looking up into his eyes. There was something so cold about them . . . black and bottomless.

For one weird instant she had the sensation of peering straight down into his soul — and finding nothing there. The shock of it brought her back again, to his insolent gaze and the impatient set of his mouth. "How's Justin this morning?" she asked lamely.

He jerked his thumb in the direction of the house. "Asleep. Why don't you ask him yourself?" He reached down to shift gears, and her hand came down on his arm.

"Wait. I've got to ask you something important. It's about Beth."

This time there was a response in the eyes, as if something roused and warily wakened. Kelsey's fingers loosened on his arm, and her heart gave an uneasy flutter.

"Get in," he nodded.

She sat as far from him as she could without falling out of the jeep, and he drove slowly, both hands on the steering wheel, eyes straight ahead. They headed down the beach toward the concession stands and the boat docks, Neale's eyes keen upon the shadows, as if he could ferret out their darkest secrets. Kelsey sat still and waited for him to say something. At last the jeep braked to an abrupt halt. Neale shifted his body so that he was facing her and appraised her with his eyes.

"So, what do you want to know?" he asked.

Kelsey took a deep breath and plunged in. "I know everyone's saying that Beth had an accident. That she — "

"Drowned," Neale finished for her, and she realized she was looking for something in his face — remorse, sorrow, *something* — but there was nothing that hinted of any emotion. "You don't have to be so careful. Facts don't shock me at all. Besides, I've pretty much accepted it."

It was a strange kind of acceptance, Kelsey thought, as if it hadn't taken much effort on his part. "But Justin hasn't accepted it — "

"Yes, I'm sorry for Justin. And for my father. Isn't that what you want me to say? I'm sorry for anyone when tragedy comes." He leaned back into the corner and propped one foot on the edge of the seat, draping one arm across his knee. "And tragedies do happen. To all of us, sooner or later."

In spite of her windbreaker, goosebumps broke out over her arms. Kelsey rubbed them, met his level gaze, saw that his walls had gone up again. "But you don't think she drowned, do you?"

A seagull called in the distance, a lonely cry beneath the relentless rush of the waves. From somewhere far away came the solitary wail of a boat whistle.

"I think she drowned," Neale said at last. "I don't think it was an accident."

In one split second Kelsey felt all her fears congeal like ice around her heart. She scarcely trusted her voice to speak. "Then . . . you think. . . ."

"Someone killed her."

The surf roared in her head . . . or was it the wind roaring . . . or just his eyes, boring into her and through her, with that blackness that was so . . . *inhuman?* She tried to swallow over the lump in her throat. "But . . . why?"

"Why?" Neale repeated. He looked down at his hand slowly tightening into a fist. "Because she was there. Because it was a good night to push someone off a cliff. Take your pick."

Kelsey didn't like the tone of his voice, so casual, so detached. He leaned forward, very, very slowly, until his eyes were inches from hers.

"And you think she was murdered, too." His eyes were almost amused. "Don't you." It was a statement, not a question. She watched his hand loosen . . . clench . . . loosen again upon his knee.

"And it makes me wonder why you think that," he said quietly. "Why you would ever think that Beth might have been murdered."

She stared hard at a spot on the windshield, wishing she had never brought it up, never gotten into this jeep, never come to this stupid island — "I don't think anything," she said. "I'm just trying to understand it, that's all."

"Don't." He twisted back into driving position, but his hand stopped halfway to the ignition as he glanced over at her. "Don't make it your business. You'll just end up getting hurt."

Kelsey's heart tightened unmercifully. She wanted to look away from him, to jump out and run from him, but his eyes held her there, compelling her to look back. *"You'll just end up getting hurt. . . ."*

"Can we go back now?" she heard herself mumble.

He revved the jeep into action, reaching the cottage within minutes. Kelsey didn't say anything more to him, and Neale drove away without a backward glance. *"You'll just end up getting hurt. . . ."* His words hung there in the pale mist, adding another chill to the morning. She pulled her windbreaker tightly around her and sat down on the steps, trying to think. *Why is Neale so convinced that Beth's been killed?* She was glad when Donna strolled up the drive, lugging a picnic basket.

"What did you do? Clean out your whole restaurant?" She waved and was answered by Donna's contagious giggle.

"This should hold us till the beach party tonight."

"What beach party?"

"Oh, didn't the guys tell you? They have to work tonight for a party. A bunch of people from the mainland reserved the beach for some big special deal, and the law says they have to have lifeguards there."

"So why are *we* going?"

Donna's eyes twinkled. "We're dates. Don't tell me you haven't been asked yet —"

"Donna!" Kelsey shook her head. "What are you up to?"

"Nothing, I swear. Only sometimes Justin's just so shy he needs a little help, is all. Isn't that right, Justin?"

Kelsey spun around, startled, as Justin came

down the front steps. He looked sleepy, his hair still rumpled, and embarrassed at having been caught.

"'Morning, sleeping beauty," Donna teased him. "Aren't you a little late this morning?"

Justin nodded. "Guess I overslept. Have you seen Neale?"

"I passed him on my way. He's got East Beach today, he said. And by the way, isn't there something you wanted to ask Kelsey? About tonight?"

"Donna!" Kelsey turned on her, but Donna only laughed and gave her a big wink.

"The beach party," Donna prompted him. "Bringing along a date. Stuff like that."

A sheepish look crept over Justin's face. "You're doing such a good job, Donna, I thought I'd let *you* ask her for me."

Donna was totally unruffled. "I did. And she said yes."

"Oh, Donna," Kelsey groaned, and Justin tossed her a quick grin as he ran by.

"See you later!" Donna called and pulled firmly on Kelsey's arm. "Come on, I know this great little place — we can eat and get some sun and eat and talk and eat — "

"You're impossible." Kelsey couldn't stay annoyed with her when she giggled like that. "And pretty presumptuous."

"Who, me? No, the word is *perceptive*, I think. I've seen the way Justin acts around you, in case *you* haven't."

"Justin's got too much going on in his life

right now to even be thinking straight," Kelsey said absently. "Especially about me. Or girls in general."

"And what are *you* thinking about?" Donna asked, peering at her intently. "Besides Justin, I mean. That look is awfully serious."

"Donna," Kelsey began, and saw her friend staring back at her in concern, as she reached out for Donna's hand. "Donna, I'm really scared."

"Kelsey, what is it —"

"Something's going on that I don't understand. I've got to tell you."

Donna nodded, her face full of questions, but she kept them to herself until they reached the picnic spot hidden back beyond the dunes. Kelsey frowned when she saw the lighthouse rising, spectrelike, on the cliffs behind them.

"Do you believe in that legend?" she asked, helping Donna unpack the basket. "About the drowned souls luring people to their deaths?" She shaded her eyes and looked up at the rotting tower tilting above them.

Donna followed her gaze. "I don't know. I think probably someone started it to keep trespassers away. I expect it could just crumble away anytime. But it still looks kind of noble, don't you think? Like some brave last stand against time?" She chuckled and took out a plastic jug and cups. "The floors have all pretty much collapsed, I think. No telling what kind of critters are holed up in there — "she shuddered. "I've always had this fear, you know, that one granddaddy of a storm could do the whole thing in."

With an effort Kelsey wrenched her eyes away. For just one second she'd had that creepy feeling again of being watched.

"You're the only one I can trust, Donna," Kelsey said, staring straight at her. "I think something awful is going on." She took a shallow breath. "I don't think Beth had an accident."

"What?" Donna sat up, rocked back on her bare heels and rested her palms on her knees. "You're really starting to scare me now, Kelsey — you better tell me everything."

So Kelsey did — beginning with her first day on the island and the notes she had gotten from Beth . . . the one frightening note with its message of death . . . the laughter in the lighthouse . . . her meeting with Isaac and his strange conversation . . . someone being in her room . . . Isaac waiting for her again outside in the dark . . . her discovery that Beth's note was missing, and finally her realization that someone had listened in on the phone. Donna sat there, eyes huge, lips slightly parted, never saying a word, not even moving, and Kelsey gave a long sigh to show she had finished.

"What should I do, Donna? I feel like I should tell someone about the note. I've felt so guilty about it ever since I found it — but I wasn't sure it was *real*, and I didn't want to get everybody all upset — "

Donna's head moved, puppetlike. "Especially since they all think it was an accident."

"And now I can't do *anything* about it."
Kelsey looked miserable. "I can't just go to
Eric, can I? Or the sheriff? You said yourself
he'd think we're crazy — he'll want proof and
I haven't got any."

"Oh, God. . . . " Donna mumbled and suddenly her eyes went twice their normal size —
"Oh, God, Kelsey . . . if it wasn't an accident
. . . do *you* think someone killed her?"

Kelsey avoided Donna's stare and scooped up
a handful of sand, letting it sift slowly through
her fingers. "Neale does," she said.

"Neale, of course," Donna snorted. "He *would*
think that. It's in keeping with his character."
Her attempt at humor fell flat, and she ducked
her head, chewing thoughtfully on some wind-
blown wisps of hair.

"But if he's right, Donna." Two sets of eyes
lifted . . . met . . . held. . . .

A warm breeze sighed around them, shape-
shifting the dunes that closed them off from the
beach, but not the lighthouse. Kelsey forced
herself not to look at it.

She still had that feeling.

Like someone was up there, watching them.

Oblivious, Donna opened some yogurt and
shook her head. "Who would kill Beth? And
why? Beth was so sweet, she wouldn't have hurt
anybody, so why would anyone want to . . . ?"
Her hands fluttered uselessly, as if to pluck
answers from the air.

Kelsey's mind raced — back through the
events of last night, the agreement she'd made
with Neale — and finally she gave in. "Listen.

You don't know everything about what happened last night."

"Oh, no. What do you mean?" Donna seemed to physically brace herself against another onslaught.

"Neale said Justin was just carried away by the undertow," Kelsey said slowly. "But Justin's a lifeguard, right? He'd know better than to go in the water if it was dangerous. He said himself East Beach is his favorite beach — he must know everything about it."

"I thought about that," Donna admitted, "but Justin didn't argue with Neale so. . . ." She shrugged, looking totally baffled.

"No, Justin didn't say anything then — but later on he told me he'd felt something grab him and pull him under. And," she went on reluctantly, "I felt something bump against me, too. And there was something in the water."

Donna went stiff all over. "You don't mean — a shark! Oh, God, Kelsey, if you saw a shark I'll just — "

"That's just it," Kelsey said miserably, "I *know* I saw something and it *looked* like a fin — but Neale says maybe it wasn't — that *real* sharkskin would have cut me — and it *was* dark out there, and I *was* pretty scared — "

Donna nodded slowly. "What about Justin? Did he see anything? Anything at all?"

Kelsey shook her head. "But Donna, the more I think about it, the weirder it gets. What if Neale was right? Would we have both been that lucky — *both* of us — if there *was* a shark out there? I mean, what are the chances of a shark coming after both of us and not attacking?"

Donna's eyes narrowed. "What are you getting at?"

"I mean, what if someone was just trying to scare us? I don't know how they did it — but — what if somehow they made it *look* like a shark attack?"

Donna's burst of laughter was completely humorless. "Why on earth would anyone do that?"

"I don't know. . . ." She stared down at the growing pile of sand beneath her fingers, but what she saw instead was the wet beach in the moonlight, and Justin sprawled there, gasping for breath, his eyes glazed with fear, his growing panic over Neale. *"Where was he when I went in the water . . . you don't understand . . . Neale . . . where were you . . . Neale. . . ."*

"I think I know," Donna said quietly, and Kelsey watched as mingled amazement and horror crept over her face. "Oh, Kelsey . . . I. . . ."

"Donna, tell me — "

"Maybe they weren't after Justin, Kelsey. Maybe they were after you."

Fear gripped her with icy tentacles. She stared at Donna, the world receding around her in a curious haze. Donna leaned forward, her hands gripping Kelsey's knee.

"Kelsey, you're the one who had Beth's note. You're the one who had some proof that she might have been killed — "

"But I don't have it anymore," Kelsey moaned. "Someone — oh, Donna — "

"Are you thinking what I'm thinking?"

"It has to be him. Everything points to him."

"Isaac," Donna whispered.

"He knew I was staying with them," Kelsey said dully. "He knew about Beth . . . he told me she was dead. And it must have been him who listened in on my phone call with Jenny . . . Neale said Isaac had just been in Eric's house to use the phone — he probably picked it up while I was on the line — and then he searched my room . . . and took Beth's note."

Donna reached out, her cold fingers clamping around Kelsey's wrist. "But you said he *denied* killing her, even though — "

"Well, what's he gonna do, turn himself in for murder? You said yourself he's the one who found the drowning victims on the beach. Didn't anyone ever *suspect* anything — "

Donna looked distraught. "Oh, they questioned him, but he always had an alibi, and I don't think anyone ever really *believed* there was foul play involved! I just don't get it — why would Isaac go around killing women? And even if he *did*, then why would he stay on the island where they could catch him? It doesn't make sense — "

"Then why was he on the beach last night after Justin's accident?" Kelsey asked tersely. "Why was he sneaking around and trying to break in the gate? He couldn't have gotten rid of me very easily with everyone else around — "

Donna's face was growing paler by the second. "I don't know," she moaned, and her eyes lifted suddenly to the tall tower above them, fixing it with such a look of shock that Kelsey's head snapped up.

"What's the matter?"

"Oh, God — someone's up there — someone's watching us — "

Kelsey cupped her hands around her eyes, squinting against the glare of sun and sun-bleached rock, trying to make out the top of the lighthouse amidst its crumbled stones and splintered railings. "Are you sure?"

"Someone was up there, I swear it. Not now, but he was — " Donna scrambled to her feet, grabbing the blanket, the cups, flinging everything into the basket. Kelsey had picked up the jug without even thinking and now stood watching her friend in dismay. Something came to her just then — something Neale had said only an hour ago — something that confirmed all her growing fears — *"Don't make it your business . . . you'll just end up getting hurt. . . ."*

And then it hit her.

She looked up again at the lighthouse, felt Donna grab her by the shoulders and turn her around so they were face to face.

Of course, Kelsey thought, and her mouth dropped open with the clarity of it all — *of course . . . Neale knows that someone killed Beth . . . Isaac must know that he knows . . . he was trying to kill Neale, not Justin . . . Neale and me . . . and Justin was simply a case of mistaken identity. . . .*

"Kelsey," Donna was shaking her, "we've got to tell someone about all this — we — "

"But how *can* we? We have absolutely no proof. Nobody will ever believe us."

"You can't go on now without someone knowing," Donna insisted desperately. "It's not safe for you — "

Not safe for me, Kelsey thought, *"you'll just end up getting hurt. . . . "* She stared at Donna, her face turning the color of chalk.

"If he tried something once, he might try it again," Donna said slowly. "He might just be waiting till you're alone, Kelsey — don't you *see?"*

But of course she did see . . . she saw the truth of the situation . . . saw herself caught up in a web of endless, endless fear. . . .

Donna shook her again. "Kelsey . . . that body we found — *he* must have done it — and now he knows *you know."*

Chapter 14

The lifeguard twirled the paper between his fingers.

He loved to play games, and this one was turning out just as he'd planned.

Kelsey was so pretty. And so gullible.

So easy to scare.

He'd had fun writing that note and leaving it under her pillow, and he'd had fun slipping into her room and taking it back again.

She was even prettier when she was frightened.

They all were, really.

He got a kick out of their fear and their helplessness and the slow, desperate way they eventually realized he was after them. . . .

Except for Beth. . . .

Beth had ruined everything because she'd come after *him*. . . .

And he didn't *want* to kill her, but he *had* to, because she *knew*. . . .

He pressed his hands to his head, squeezing

. . . squeezing . . . until the mixed-up darkness began to fade from his mind.

And then he read the note one more time.

Kelsey . . . I think someone is going to kill me. . . .

The lifeguard laughed to himself and set the notepaper on fire, watching it burn to a soft gray ash.

He wouldn't hurry with Kelsey.

He'd just take his time and enjoy it.

Chapter 15

Kelsey dragged her feet through the sand. Donna had gone on to work promising to see her tonight at the party, where they could talk some more. Until then Kelsey knew her own mind would be a blur. She could hardly even concentrate now, and swore to herself as she suddenly tripped over someone's foot and fell forward.

"Excuse me, lady, but we don't allow accidents on this beach." A pair of strong arms righted her, and she found herself looking up into Skip's grin. "I suggest you get your own personal lifeguard. I recommend myself."

Kelsey disentangled herself and couldn't help laughing. "What are you doing here?"

"I work here, remember?" He tipped his cap and steered her to a hot dog stand. "What's your pleasure?"

"For breakfast?"

Skip wiggled his eyebrows. "Trust me — you won't regret this." He pushed his way to the counter, and Kelsey leaned back against the wall.

"Hi."

She jumped, her cheek brushing against Justin's, and felt his hand slide across her back, leaving warm tingles where he touched.

"Hi, yourself." *Oh, Justin, I wish I could tell you what's happening but I'm afraid and I don't have any proof and you've been through so much already. . . .* "I'm having — uh — breakfast."

"So I see." He looked slightly incredulous as Skip returned and handed her a hot dog. It promptly gushed a huge glob of mustard onto Justin's bare feet, and he tried to rub it off into the sand. "Sorry I was in such a hurry this morning," Justin said. "How was your picnic?"

Skip looked up around a mouthful of bun. "Disastrous if Donna made it." He waved his last bite of hot dog and started off. "Gotta get back. See you tonight, huh?"

Justin took Kelsey's hot dog and tossed it into a litter can. "Poison. Got any plans for today?"

"Just walking."

"Good. You can walk me back to my station." They waved as Skip's jeep made a swerve at them and disappeared back down the beach.

"Donna shouldn't have said what she did this morning." She looked up sideways, at his brown hair, the rich deep tan, the long, thick lashes. . . .

"Yes, she should've. I *was* going to ask you. She didn't trap me."

"But I thought you guys are supposed to be working. Are you allowed to have dates?"

"Technically? No. But when Skip happens to know who's giving the party, he makes sure people like you and Donna get invited. Don't worry. We'll just tell everyone you're part of the Beach Patrol."

"Sounds like a bad sitcom," Kelsey laughed. She loved hearing Justin laugh, too — loved the easy way it came out, bringing new lights to his blue eyes. Hearing him laugh like that, she could almost believe that everything was all right. . . .

"By the way, Dad and your mom took off for the mainland." Justin's eyes scanned the ocean as they walked. "She said she forgot to tell you." He put his hands on her shoulders and smiled down at her. "Well, this is where I get off. You coming to the beach later?"

Kelsey answered evasively. "I don't know. I may stop in the village for a while . . . do some shopping."

"I give free lessons," Justin reminded her. There was teasing behind his innocent expression, and Kelsey punched him lightly on the chest.

"In what?"

"Why, swimming, of course!" Justin looked askance. "What were *you* thinking of?"

Kelsey could still feel him — the gentle pressure of his hands upon her shoulders, his chin softly brushing her forehead — all the way up the beach she could still feel him, and it warmed her all over. She kept walking, thinking of his smile, his soft-spoken voice, his laugh, until she suddenly realized she had reached the end of the beach.

For one disoriented moment Kelsey stood there. Off to her right lay the ocean, to her left a clutter of bars and shops. In the distance she could see the mainland, and straight ahead of her the ferry landing. Kelsey dropped her eyes to the boats docked just below where she was standing. She smiled, sniffing the air — the salt and fish and old, wet wood — and felt her smile freeze upon her lips.

Isaac was coming out of a houseboat.

He didn't see her standing just above him, gazing down with a look of fear. He limped across the pier and gestured to another old man who seemed to be waiting for him, and together they climbed into an open boat, and putted away.

Without thinking, Kelsey went down the first flight of steps she came to, walking out onto a narrow wooden ramp that paralleled the larger pier up above. She went slowly, keeping her eyes on that boat pulling away, watching as it went around the curve of the beach and disappeared. Her heart was pounding.

She was standing right beside Isaac's houseboat.

There didn't seem to be anyone else around — not anyone or anything — save for the bad smell that hung in the air. A graveyard, Kelsey thought suddenly, a graveyard for stinking, forgotten, old, old things. . . . Swallowing hard, she swung herself up onto Isaac's deck, then ducked down again quickly, through the hatch, praying that nobody had stayed behind to wait for him.

The place was a pigsty. Kelsey pressed her sleeve against her nose, holding her breath. Moldy food lay everywhere. There was a rumpled cot with a filthy sheet that looked like it had never been changed. Empty liquor bottles covered the greasy floor, the lingering odor of whiskey mingling with the stink of stale urine and sweat. *You must be crazy, coming here . . . you must be out of your mind . . . suppose he comes back . . . suppose he saw you and right now he's creeping up on deck. . . .*

A sudden creaking made her scream — she put her hand to her mouth and backed up, feeling the boat groan beneath her feet. It wasn't safe here — she had to get out. The floor tilted, and she whirled around to the old brass-bound chest to steady herself against it.

The first thing she saw was the knife.

Kelsey had never seen a knife that long or that ugly. Something thick had dried on the blade and had never been cleaned off, and the point looked dull and nearly blunted. Whoever felt the tip of this knife would die a slow, painful death. . . .

In mingled horror and fascination she leaned forward. Now she could see something else there, puddled beneath the knife — something dark . . . dark red. . . .

She reached out to touch it.

Something stuck to her fingers and clung as

she drew back in alarm — something that streamed and flowed and ran down her arm. . . .

Only it wasn't blood.

It was a scarf.

A long, red scarf that she had seen before. In a picture on the mantel in Eric's cottage.

Beth had been wearing it around her neck.

"No. . . . " Kelsey whispered, "Oh, no. . . . "

There was a scurrying in the corner, and she wheeled around, screaming again as a huge, mangy rat fixed her with shining eyes.

Kelsey dropped the scarf and ran.

Chapter 16

What am I going to do? Kelsey slammed the cottage door and leaned breathlessly against it. *Go to the sheriff? Tell him he can go right down and pick up his murderer?* No, Donna was probably her best bet, only Donna was working and she wouldn't see her till tonight. For a second, Kelsey thought of going over to the restaurant, then remembered she didn't know the name of it or how to get there. Should she finally tell Justin what was going on? Neale? He'd be furious with her, she knew, but at least he already believed that Beth had been murdered. Skip? But he would only accuse her of playing another joke on him. . . .

Going to the mantel, Kelsey picked up the photograph, staring at Beth and the red scarf. She hadn't made a mistake. She knew the scarf was Beth's. She knew Isaac had killed her. But *why?*

"You'll just end up getting hurt. . . ."

She could call the sheriff. Leave an anonymous tip, then hang up before anyone could trace the call. She went into the kitchen and reached for the phone. It rang just as her hand closed around it, jolting her out of her skin.

"Kelsey? Hello? Is anybody there?"

Kelsey's hands were shaking so badly that she could hardly hold the receiver. "Mom? Is that you? Oh, Mom, I've got to tell you — "

"Listen, honey, I only have a second. Eric's in the hospital. Kelsey, can you hear me? I said Eric is — "

"I hear you," Kelsey said numbly. "What happened?"

"The doctors don't think it's anything serious — he collapsed, but he's resting now."

"Collapsed — "

"His heart, honey. They're sure it's from all the strain, but they want to keep him a couple days. Just to make sure. Will you tell the boys?"

"They're not here right now. Nobody's here but me — "

" — the shock, Kelsey. It's just too much. But we'll be fine, huh? Try to have some fun and don't worry."

The click came, and Kelsey stood there, staring down at the phone. Tell the boys. Just like that. *Your dad had a heart attack and I've found your sister's murderer. Great Kelsey, just great.*

She forced herself back to the beach, surprised at how cloudy it was. She hunched her shoulders against the wind, and when she spotted the jeep coming towards her, she ran up and waved it down.

"Where's the fire?" Skip grinned.

"Not exactly a fire," she said anxiously. "Eric's in the hospital."

"You're kidding." Skip's mouth dropped open. "Is it bad?"

"No, but they're keeping him a few days."

"His heart again?"

Kelsey nodded, meeting Skip's grim expression with one of her own. "I'm on my way to find Justin now. I think Neale's on East Beach — do you know how I can get ahold of him?"

Skip made a dismissive gesture. "Not to worry. Justin's over there, too, helping him with something — I'll call them right now."

She smiled at him, relief flooding through her. "I didn't want to have to . . . tell them. . . ."

"I know." Skip's eyes clouded over almost angrily. "It's a damn shame. How much *more* can happen?"

If you only knew, Kelsey thought — *tell him — tell him now — make him call the sheriff and go to Isaac's houseboat* — "Skip —"

"See you later, huh?" Skip squeezed her arm, leaving her with half-formed words on her lips as he sped away.

Kelsey dragged herself back to Eric's cottage and stretched out on the couch, staring again at the picture on the mantel. Beth's smile was so sweet, so touching . . . so much like Justin's — the same gentleness, the same shyness — *why do the innocent ones always have to suffer . . . ?* She threw her arm across her eyes, trying to shut out the image of the deer hanging on Skip's wall, trying to stay awake . . . to keep the voice away. . . .

"Don't struggle . . . it'll be easier if you don't struggle. . . . "

And the roaring came again, like it always did, that growing surge of indistinct sound and a scream, muffled, distant. . . .

"Don't struggle. . . . "

But she was struggling . . . great gasps of air from lungs bursting, and that split second, that terrifying instant of realization as strength gave out and water poured in, black and sickening and endless. . . .

"Don't. . . . " the voice fading as everything faded, as her very life faded . . . ended. . . .

"I'm trying to hold on, Dad — I'm trying — "

She cried out, starting up off the couch, vaguely aware of the knocking which had called her back to consciousness.

The room was dark and murky; twilight oozing past the windows. She inched toward the door, keeping flat against the wall, trying to peer out onto the porch without being seen. Was that a laugh she had heard just then? Visions of Isaac swept through her mind — the knife — the huge rat watching her as she tried to run — if Isaac was out there now . . . if he knew she was alone. . . .

The sound came again, and Kelsey saw the tree limb slapping at the window. Inching open the door, she frowned at the swaying trees, the heavy smell of rain.

She was surprised at how late it was: half past six. Almost as an afterthought she grabbed her purple windbreaker on her way out; it might get cold later on. She wondered where everyone was, where the party was supposed to be. Noticing lights flickering farther up the beach, she headed toward them.

Justin ran up to her before she even reached the party site.

"Where *were* you? I was getting ready to call out the National Guard — " He was trying to joke, but he looked worried.

Kelsey felt touched by his concern. "I fell asleep — "

"But I looked in your room — "

"No, Eric's cottage. Sorry, guess I should have left a note or something."

Emotions struggled across his face, and he got them quickly under control. "It's just that . . . with all that's happened. . . . "

"I know. It's okay." She wasn't prepared for his arms going around her, drawing her against him. She closed her eyes and slipped her arms around his waist. He was trembling.

"If anything ever happened to you. . . . " He left the sentence unfinished, and Kelsey leaned against him, his heartbeat beneath her cheek.

"If you two can tear yourselves away from each other," Skip came up, wiping sweat from his eyes, "there's lots to do back there — "

Justin fell into step beside him and swung Kelsey around, his arm still draped around her neck. "Any news about Dad?"

Kelsey shook her head. "No news is good news."

"I guess," Justin conceded, then sighed. "I don't know about you, but I'm really not up to this tonight — "

"What?" Skip's mouth dropped open. "Now Justin, *no* one is *ever* too tired to party! It'll cure all your troubles! And besides, you get paid time and a half."

"Is Donna here?" Kelsey was craning her neck, trying to locate her friend, but there were too many people on the beach.

The party site had been set up by the second lifeguard station, a fair distance away from the lighthouse, but still close enough to see the scarred cliffs in between glimpses of the moon. The sky had really clouded up. There were no stars, and a restless breeze chopped at the waves.

"We need to turn those floodlights on," Justin peered inland, and Skip followed his gaze.

"Okay, but I don't think they'll do much good."

"Well, the fire'll help some, I guess." Justin watched as Skip disappeared through the crowd, and several minutes later two tall light poles, practically hidden by trees, burst into feeble illumination. Justin studied them for several seconds, then turned as an invisible someone called his name. "I guess you'll have to mingle without me for a while." He smiled down at Kelsey, but his face still looked tired.

"Don't worry about me, I'm a great mingler."

"That's what I *will* worry about," Justin tossed back, and Kelsey set out to find Donna.

The beach was beautiful by firelight. Kelsey stood back, entranced by the huge camp fire blazing up into the night, the sand glowing like fallen embers, the cliffs gleaming like mounded ash. Beyond the blare of music came the sounds of dancing and singing, the sizzle of wood and food cooking, and the whine of the wind.

"Donna!" Kelsey raised her hand and maneuvered her way over to where Donna was pulling a can of soda from an ice tub. "There you are! I — " Kelsey felt her greeting die as she caught a glimpse of Donna's face. It was red and puffy from crying, and even now she looked like she might cry again. "Donna — what's — "

"Oh, Skip and I had a fight. Nothing unusual — "

"But I just saw him — he didn't seem upset — "

"He never does. I'm going to dance with every guy at this party. I'm never going to speak to him again." She sounded hurt and angry, and Kelsey reached out for her.

"Donna, I'm sorry about you and Skip — but I have to talk to you. Can you forget it for just five minutes? I have *proof* that Isaac killed Beth — "

"You *what?*"

They hurried past the crowd, past the lights, forming a tight little huddle among the trees and dunes.

"Donna, listen to me. You know that picture on the mantel at Eric's? The one of the family?" To each question, Donna nodded, and Kelsey rushed on. "The scarf Beth was wearing — *Isaac has that scarf!* Oh, Donna don't you see — "

"Where?" Donna broke in, her face stunned. "How do you know?"

"Because I saw it. In his houseboat."

Donna's eyes nearly bulged out of her head. "What!?"

"Oh, Donna, I know I shouldn't have, but I couldn't help it! I had to!"

"I have to sit down," Donna said weakly. She stared up at Kelsey as if her friend had gone mad.

"I'm not crazy, I really did go — "

"Oh, Lord — "

"There was a knife there. *This long,* I swear to God. And Beth's scarf right beside it."

"Beth's. . . . "

"We've got to tell somebody. People have to know that Beth didn't just have an accident. They have to know that there's a murderer loose on the island — "

"Well, what are you gonna do? Tell the sheriff?" Donna looked totally dumbfounded. Her can of soda turned over, draining into the sand.

"I thought . . . I'd tell Neale."

"Neale! Why on earth — "

"Donna, I told you before, Neale's the only one who believes something bad happened to Beth. Maybe the sheriff will listen to him if he tells him about Isaac — "

A voice that wasn't Donna's asked quietly, "Tells him *what* about Isaac?"

They stared at each other, frozen. Neale and Justin and Skip were all standing beside the path, watching them, their faces blank with disbelief.

"I can't believe you two," Skip mumbled. "You're really something."

"How dare you spy on us!" Donna shouted, struggling for her dignity. Neale's look suggested that he would dare anything he damn well pleased. "How rude!" she added lamely.

For a second Kelsey thought Neale was actually going to laugh, which made it even worse.

"Isaac did it," she raised her chin defiantly. "He killed Beth. I know he did."

Justin looked stunned.

Neale nodded, more to himself than to her. "He confessed, I suppose."

"Of course he didn't confess!" Kelsey blurted out. "*He* says he didn't do it but that he knows who *did!* But he's lying!"

"What proof?" Neale demanded.

Kelsey's voice dropped. "Beth's scarf. It was lying on his trunk, beside a knife with bloodstains on it."

"A knife with . . ." Neale's lips twitched in a humorless smile. "Of course, I see now. Solid concrete evidence."

Skip threw back his head and hooted with laughter. "Fish blood! You girls are just too much!"

"It was *hers*," Kelsey snapped, but her tone had grown less confident. "It *was*. The scarf. The one she had on in that picture. . . . "

Justin was just staring, as if words had completely deserted him.

Neale studied the ground. The dunes. The

brief glow of moon through passing clouds. "Yes . . . well . . . I imagine Beth was the only one in the world who had a red scarf."

Kelsey heard Donna make a sound in her throat. Her own face began to burn. "I can't believe you're all being so *cold* about this. I thought you'd — "

Neale's hand came out of the darkness so fast, closed around her arm so tightly that she gasped.

"You don't know *anything* about this. Not *anything*. Maybe the scarf wasn't even *hers*; nobody knows what she had on that night. Or maybe it *was* hers. Or maybe Isaac found it after she was already lying out on the rocks somewhere. Did you ever think of that?"

"Well . . . no . . . but — "

"And maybe you can tell the sheriff you went breaking and entering and trying to cause trouble for people — hell, I'm surprised you didn't just *take* the scarf! Then they could have got you for burglary, too!"

Kelsey was shaking, partly from anger, partly from fear at his outburst. Donna hadn't uttered a word. Kelsey wondered if she had fainted.

"I . . . thought . . . you'd at least . . . care," she managed to stammer, and felt a jolt through her body as Neale shook her.

"You don't *know* what I care about," he seethed. "You don't *know* what I feel or what — " A strange look crossed his face then, made him pause . . . stop . . . as if he had momentarily lost his train of thought. It was a look she couldn't quite identify: Fear? Surprise? Regret at having said too much? He released her almost roughly and stalked away, but it was several more minutes before anyone spoke.

Skip began to chuckle, softly at first, then louder until he finally reached up to wipe his eyes. "You crazy girls — Kelsey Holmes and Doctor Donna — " He shook his head, still laughing as he walked away, and Justin looked down, his voice strangely tight.

"Look . . . Kelsey. . . . "

"Oh, just go away and leave me alone." She went over to Donna, refusing to look at him, and at last he turned and went back. to the beach.

"Yeah, well, thanks for nothing, you jerks!" Donna kicked furiously at the sand, groaning as she stubbed her toe. Kelsey just stood there and watched her. "We should have known better — at least I thought *Justin* would believe us — but — oh, forget it, who needs them anyway?" She retrieved her empty can with one angry swipe. "Try to help, and this is what you get. What's the matter with them, anyway — you'd think they didn't want to know the truth! Like they're all so protective of Isaac all of a sudden!" she sputtered. "Like they're all so *convinced* that Isaac couldn't have done it! And how would *they* know anyway?"

Kelsey didn't answer.

She gazed out into the flickering darkness, at the glare of the fire, the patina of the sea . . . but what she saw instead was that strange, dark look on Neale's face that chilled her soul.

Chapter 17

The lifeguard stood in the shadows, oblivious to the noise and the laughter on the beach.

They shouldn't be here — they had no right — this was *his* beach and there was so much to do. . . .

He stared down at his fists and saw that they were shaking.

Isaac! Isaac knew who did it!

He would be sad to have to kill him, of course — he really *liked* Isaac — but he didn't really have a choice now.

And Kelsey . . . well . . . it would only be a matter of time and she'd figure it out. . . .

Kelsey was too smart for her own good.

People like that just ended up getting hurt. . . .

He covered his face with his hands and felt the cold sweat pouring off him. He always felt like this — sick and sad and empty — when it was time for the game to be over. When it was time to do what he had to do.

Like last summer with Rebecca . . . after all

the planning, the waiting . . . and it had been
so *easy*, luring her into the water like that. . . .

It had been one of his best tricks.

He smiled and started toward the light, a
noiseless shadow, invisible in the crowd.

Tonight. He'd get them both tonight.

Poor Kelsey. . . .

No lifeguard could save her now.

Chapter 18

"I don't like the looks of that sky," Justin squinted against the wind, forcing his hair back from his eyes.

"I don't, either," Neale agreed. "Did anyone hear a weather report?"

"Chance of a storm, but not till tomorrow — " Skip stiffened in his chair, gave a sharp blast on his whistle. "Hey! You two clowns over there, cut it out right now! You want to get yourselves killed?"

Kelsey and Donna exchanged looks as Neale and Justin ran off to break up a fight in the water. After a brief struggle in which the perpetrators were separated, Skip semed satisfied and settled down again. Donna eyed him acidly.

"No beer? Or is your whistle spiked?"

"My *dear*, I'm on *duty*," Skip reminded her self-righteously.

"Well, I'm *off* duty. Permanently." She marched away, and Skip held up his megaphone, shouting after her.

"Yeah, well, why don't you fix up your attitude while you're at it, huh?"

"Shut up, Skip!"

"Don't test me, Donna — don't even *think* about making me jealous, you hear? It won't work! You're dead if you do!"

Kelsey gasped, staring up into his face. It looked eerie and unnatural, half in and out of shadow. "Do you think it *will* storm?" She hurried to change the subject, folding her arms around one of the wooden posts, staring up at the mass of thick darkness. She would have preferred never talking to any of them again, but a feeling of uneasiness had settled over her, one she couldn't seem to shake, and the boiling clouds overhead weren't helping any.

"Hey — " Skip's hand came down, patting her head. "Don't worry about it. We got three lifeguards here — one of us'll save you, I promise."

She ignored the remark. "Any bathrooms around here?"

"If you mean those wonderful little portable outhouses, they're back there." Skip pointed toward a cluster of dunes and added, "Need an escort?"

"Thanks, but I thought you came with someone else."

She turned away, but his voice stopped her. "Kelsey?"

She was surprised at the look on his face — gentle, almost embarrassed, and definitely un-Skiplike. "Look . . . about what happened back there. I shouldn't have laughed, and I'm sorry.

I know you're only trying to help. You've been . . . well . . . good for Justin. For all of us. I'm real glad you're here."

She didn't know what to say. She saw his shoulders squaring, as if adjusting himself back into his old personality, and he stood up and made a bow.

"The great one has spoken," he said.

"I believe he has." She smiled at him and turned back to the path.

She was glad there wasn't a line at the bathroom, but it was scary back there so far from the light with no people around. When she started down the footpath again she tried to avoid the shadows, unsettled by the swaying palms and their deceptive patterns underfoot. She wished she knew where Donna had gone. She could hardly tell where the rocks ended and the darkness began . . . the rocks . . . so bulky and bowed . . . like nighttime creatures hulking there, waiting to step out and grab her.

And then one did.

Kelsey felt the sudden hold on her wrist, saw the black shape lunge between her and the sky, felt the scream rise in her throat and strangle her as relentless hands pressed hard over her mouth. She reeled backward, gagging as the sour stench of whiskey and vomit overwhelmed her.

"Won't do you no good screaming, girl." She felt his rancid breath in her ear, down her neck. "I'll be gone so quick, they'll think you're crazy for sure."

Kelsey's whole body thudded, one giant, racing heartbeat.

"I seed you go in there, to my place. I knowed you looked around." His voice exploded in a gleeful laugh, shrill and singsonglike. " 'Cause Isaac has eyes in the back of his head . . . 'cause Isaac has eyes in the back of his head!" She groaned and struggled, but he slammed her hard against him. "You think I done her in, don't you? I know what you think, and I know what I saw. And you better not waste your time barking after old Isaac, little girl — you'd best be worrying about yourself!"

Kelsey thought her neck would snap; he was bending her head back, slowly, slowly, till all at once she could see the greasy eye patch and the puckered ridges across his face. His breath hit her again, making her swoon.

"You know too much," he hissed. "So have a care, girl. Why, I'm just likely to find *you* some fine mornin', washed right up on that beach like all the others — "

Kelsey bit him. With one quick jerk she twisted her mouth free and brought her teeth down on his hand, tasting blood. With a cry of pain, Isaac staggered back, and Kelsey hurtled toward the beach, screaming at the top of her lungs.

"Justin! Justin! Somebody help me!"

And at first she thought it was *her* screams resounding in the far corners of her frenzied brain . . . *her* voice bouncing off the rocks, coming back at her in stereophonic panic —

"Help — *Somebody help!"*

She stopped, totally confused. Behind her, the path was empty. Ahead of her the party was going on, oblivious to her cries. But someone besides herself had been screaming . . . was still screaming . . . even now. . . .

"*Help — drowning — help —* "

It was far away yet terrifyingly close, that awful sound, water being gulped down . . . choked back up . . . arms thrashing . . . helpless . . . mad with terror. . . .

Kelsey's eyes went wide. Sobbing, she ran for shore — *My God, where is she?*

"*Help — help me —* "

Where was *everybody — couldn't they hear?* "Help!" Kelsey shrieked, hating the sudden silence, worse than the screams. "Where *are* you?"

Something broke surface . . . flailing . . . struggling. . . . In a daze of horror Kelsey saw the arms come out of the water — ghostly in a sliver of moonlight . . . and they reached for her . . . and went under. . . .

"Justin!" She raced toward the lights, and she was still screaming, screaming, she didn't think she had ever stopped screaming . . . "*Justin!*"

But someone had seen her now. Someone, at last, had seen her, people running, gathering around her — Skip from one direction — Justin from another — Neale from still another. . . . It was Neale who reached her first, who caught her, trying to decipher the gibberish that spilled from her lips.

"Hurry — someone's drowning — "

"What?" Her teeth rattled as he shook her. "Kelsey, *where?* Are you sure?"

"I'm sure — I heard her — I heard her — "

She felt Neale's slap across her cheek, heard Justin telling him to stop and Neale snapping something back, and Skip and all of them running, and she was running, too, leading them to the spot where she had seen the body go down. . . .

They left her on shore, and she watched them in a hazy blur, diving in, swimming out. Someone — Skip, she thought — ran to call for a rescue crew, but was back again so quickly she thought she must have only imagined he'd gone. And everyone was running out now — the party stopping — word spread by invisible waves of fear. They stood around watching, waiting, as the waves buffeted the lifeguards around like so many broken shells.

"I can't find her!" Justin cried.

"Leave it!" Skip's voice swelled above the surf, joined by the deeper shouts of Neale.

"The rescue's here, Justin! Leave it! Swim back!"

"NO!"

Someone grabbed Kelsey's arm — she swung around and stared into Donna's frightened eyes. They held onto each other without speaking. Silence stretched on and on, until Neale shouted again, pleading, "Justin! Come on — you can't do any more — "

For as long as she lived she would never forget Justin's voice then, the uncontrollable desperation echoing back to them through the wind and the water.

"I can't *find* her, Neale — I can't find *any-one* — "

"Justin! Come back!"

"Neale — somebody — for God's sake, *I can't find her!*"

Chapter 19

"I don't believe it. I just don't believe it." Skip hung up the phone and turned to face them, his expression baffled.

"Are you sure?" Neale asked again. "Are *they* sure?"

Justin stared at the floor, as if it had hypnotized him.

"They've checked and double-checked." Skip fell with a thump into his chair and took an absentminded sip of coffee. "They say it's a mess over there; everybody still has a different story about what happened. Most of them still think it was a joke, and they're mad 'cause it ruined their party."

Donna squeezed Kelsey's arm, but they kept quiet.

"Nobody's missing," Skip said incredulously. "Nobody's missing and nobody's *reported* anyone missing."

"It's a mistake then," Donna said flatly. "They've made a mistake — "

"Oh, Donna, don't be stupid," Skip shot back.

"If Kelsey saw someone, then there *was* someone!"

The silence was electric. Kelsey lifted her face from her hands and looked accusingly at each of the boys in turn.

"I know what you're thinking." Now their eyes were on her; only Justin had the grace to look halfway guilty. "I didn't imagine it. It was as real as any of you. I heard someone scream, and I heard someone fighting for her life."

Neale's mouth tightened into a thin line. "How do you know it was a her?"

"Because it *sounded* like a her!" Kelsey nearly shouted. "I heard her, and I saw her go down! I don't care what you say!"

"This happened before," Donna said softly.

Everyone stared at her, reluctantly.

"Come on," Skip said too quickly, too lightly. "You can't — "

"It did happen before." Justin shook his head slowly, staring at some inner memory. "That other lifeguard — Rebecca — the night she drowned, she heard someone drowning, too . . . only. . . . "

The silence stretched on forever, until Neale suddenly filled it. "Only there wasn't anybody there. Except Rebecca. Yeah, I've heard all that garbage — what are you bringing all that up again for?" But he looked uneasy and shifted his eyes away.

"I saw someone," Kelsey whispered.

Skip seemed fascinated by an invisible spot on the ceiling. He watched it for quite a long while before he spoke again. "But that was the sheriff that just called back, Kelsey, and he said —"

"She *knows* what he said, Skip, she's not *deaf!*" Donna snapped.

Kelsey jumped up from the couch, flinging away Justin's arm. He looked slightly stunned, but her pride forced her on out the front door and across the yard to the beach, where the wind and the ocean drowned out her anger. "I *hate* you!" she screamed, and she raised her fists into the air and shook them at the endless black water. "I hate you! *I'll always hate you!*"

Her knees gave out, spilling her onto the sand. "I hate you . . . I do. . . . " And still the screams came and all the memories, all hurting, all hurting at once, until there was no strength left in her whole body.

Kelsey lay there, limp and exhausted. She didn't even move when she realized that someone had sat down beside her . . . that maybe he had been sitting there for a very long time.

He handed her a handkerchief, and at last she looked up.

It was Neale.

"Go away," Kelsey said miserably. "I don't want to talk to you." She blew her nose and squeezed her eyes tightly. Already her head was beginning to throb.

"Tell me again what you saw," Neale said quietly, but Kelsey turned her face away.

"No. I've told you a million times already. Look, do you think this is my idea of a joke? That I'd put Justin — or any of you — through all this —" She broke off, and slowly got herself under control. "You . . . saw him out there tonight," she went on unevenly. "He was like a crazy person. It broke my heart."

A long silence drew out between them, beneath the low howl of the wind, and the waves crashing onto the shoreline. Kelsey shivered violently and pressed herself into the sand.

"And what else is breaking it?" Neale asked.

Kelsey stiffened, ready to defend herself with denials. But she just couldn't fight it anymore.

"My father died. Two years ago." She waited for some word of condolence, but when it didn't come she went on. "We were at the beach, and we'd gone out in the boat." She held her breath till her head felt like exploding. She exhaled slowly. "Somehow . . . the boat turned over. Dad. . . ." She swallowed painfully, her voice catching — "Dad didn't make it. He saved my life . . . but he . . . drowned."

Beside her the shadows shifted as if Neale had lowered his head. She felt his thigh against the curve of her arm.

"I still see him, you know . . . I have these dreams and they keep coming and they're so real . . . I see him reaching out to me, and telling me not to struggle, because it'll be easier if I don't fight him. . . . "

She couldn't stop the crying then, no matter how hard she tried to hold it back, but when at last she grew silent, Neale was still there.

"Well," she said at last, drawing a shaky breath, "now you know. I guess you're sorry you asked."

"And I guess I'm supposed to blame you or

feel bad for you because your father's dead and you're not. Is that it?"

Kelsey was so shocked that she raised up on her elbows. "He died trying to save me! Don't you understand? He was the kindest, the most loving —"

"A saint, yes, I see." Neale waved his hand. "Please. Spare me the details."

She gaped at him. "How can you talk like that? You don't understand at —"

"I understand," Neale said slowly, each word distinct, "that some things happen to us that we can't control. There's no explanation for them, and they never make sense, no matter how much we want them to. That whether we're good or bad they don't really have anything to do with us at all." His black eyes fixed on hers, drawing her into their depths. "I understand," he said, "that you've been given a second chance. My advice to you is don't blow it."

Kelsey felt anger surging up in her, and the look she gave him was scathing. "Well, I might just be dead by morning, thanks to you, and I hope that makes you very happy!"

"Dead!" Neale scoffed. "Of what? Feeling sorry for yourself?"

"It just might interest you to know that Isaac almost strangled me tonight!" It was out before she thought, and Neale's eyes narrowed.

"What do you mean?"

"He threatened to kill me!" she went on, but some of the boldness had gone from her voice. "He said I might wash up on the beach some morning like all the others." She shut her eyes

174

against a sudden image . . . a body . . . by the lighthouse . . . in the weeds. . . .

"Isaac said *that?*" Neale's voice sank even lower, his stare going through her like a lance.

"He saw me go on his boat today," Kelsey admitted reluctantly. "He said again that he didn't kill Beth . . . but — "

"But what?"

"What he told me before. That he knows who did."

Neale wasn't even looking at her now. He was gazing out to sea, and the wind lashed his hair, giving him a wild, frightening look. Kelsey heard his voice, carefully controlled.

"Did he say who it is?" Neale asked.

She shook her head. "No. Just that he knew. But he didn't tell me."

Something snapped on the path behind them, and Neale was on his feet so fast that Kelsey wasn't even certain she had seen him jump up.

"Relax," Skip's voice came out of the dark. "It's just us."

It was obvious that Neale didn't appreciate being eavesdropped on. He reached down and pulled Kelsey roughly to her feet, glaring at the newcomers. "What do you want?"

"We were getting worried," Donna said, annoyed at Neale's greeting.

Skip just laughed it off. "So old Isaac has the murderer picked out, huh? Well, this island is just *crawling* with smart detectives — "

"That's not funny, Skip," Donna glared at him.

"Sure it is. Almost as funny as you and

Kelsey are." Skip grabbed her arm, but Donna shook him off. "Oh, come on, be a big girl and use your head — you remember, that place where everyone else has a brain?"

"Drop dead, Skip," Donna muttered, and Kelsey stood there helplessly, watching her go.

"Donna!"

"I'll see you tomorrow!" Donna called back, strangely choked. "Are you walking on the beach in the morning?"

"Yes, but — Donna, wait!" Kelsey ran after her, only half conscious of the boys heading back to the house. "Donna — "

"It's my fault, you know — " Donna wiped angrily at her tears, tried to smile. "He's such a total jerk, and I'm so stupid — "

"No, you're not. I think Skip likes you more than you know — more than *he* knows — "

"*Now* who has an empty head?" Donna's laugh was weak, and she shivered. "Listen, can I borrow your jacket? It's a cold walk home."

"Why don't you wait a minute," Kelsey slipped out of her windbreaker, handing it over. "Let Justin give you a ride — "

"No thanks." Donna jerked the hood up over her head and dug her hands into the pockets. "See you in the morning."

Kelsey trudged back, going up to her room without seeing anyone. The boys were all in the kitchen and, she supposed, still having fun at her expense. She tried to put herself in their places, but it only made her angrier. *I'd believe Justin . . . I'd believe Justin, no matter what he told me. . . .*

The knock at her door nearly sent her out of her skin. "Who is it?" she asked, almost angrily.

"Me. Justin." Kelsey went over and opened the door, and they stood there looking at each other. There were dark circles under his eyes, a gauntness to his cheeks where the last few days had finally taken their toll. "I . . . just wanted to check on you . . . to see if — "

"If I'm still seeing things?" The words were out before she could stop them. She turned away and sat on the foot of her bed.

"Look," Justin said at last, "I don't know what happened out there tonight . . . what you saw or heard . . . I *do* know that something was wrong. That something terrified you. I guess . . . well, I guess I just went crazy for a minute, diving in and not finding anyone. I guess I just kept thinking about Beth and. . . ." His explanation trailed off, and his eyes lifted, bewildered. "I'm really sorry about your dad."

So he and Skip had heard that part, too. Kelsey stiffened as Justin crossed the room and sat down beside her. "This whole thing . . . I guess it's been like a nightmare for you."

And again she numbed her emotions, her body, her mind. It took a while to even realize that Justin's fingers had slipped beneath her chin, were tilting her head so their eyes met. *So blue . . . so beautifully blue. . . .*

"Oh, Kelsey," he whispered, and his lips met hers, his arms strong in their gentleness, wrapped around her, easing her down, holding her close, keeping her safe. . . . "Kelsey," he murmured again, and for just one brief, sweet instant, pressed against him, heartbeat to heartbeat, all her walls and defenses crumbled uselessly, finally away. . . . "Kelsey . . . I need you. . . . "

She didn't want him to stop, didn't want to leave his arms — yet she was almost relieved when Neale's footsteps sounded in the hall, bringing them back to reality.

At the door, Justin glanced over his shoulder and gave her a slow smile. "Do you think you'll be all right or should I stay?"

Her heart was fluttering so uncontrollably that she stammered. "I . . . can sleep."

"I'll see you in the morning then." He backed out of the room. "Good-night."

For a long time she lay there, staring at the door, at the place on the bed where he'd been . . . where he'd held her. . . . She climbed under the covers and switched off the lamp, smiling a little at the darkness and the chill and the rattle of the wind at the windows.

But then she pretended the blankets were Justin's arms. . . .

And all the terrible fears, all the dangers, faded away at last into a deep blue dream of Justin's eyes.

Chapter 20

The lifeguard flattened himself against the lighthouse wall, his eyes wide and fixed in terror on the rocks below.

It wasn't her!

This couldn't have happened — *couldn't have* — not to *him* — not when he'd planned so carefully. . . .

The wind was like the inside of his head, screaming and shrieking, like *she* had screamed . . . like *she* had screamed and screamed, the whole way down until she'd finally hit those rocks and lay still. . . .

He caught his breath, his own scream choking him.

It was Kelsey's fault, this terrible thing that had happened.

Kelsey's fault.

She'd said she'd be out walking this morning . . . he'd *heard* her say that . . . and he'd waited for her, oh, so patiently . . . just watched and waited for that purple windbreaker to come up the beach . . . waited and followed . . . tracking her . . . choosing the perfect moment. . . .

And he'd felt that strange, wonderful thrill, coming up behind her . . . that flow of pure invincibility . . . that strange, cold joy as she sensed him there and whirled around —

Only it wasn't Kelsey.

It wasn't Kelsey that had whirled around, eyes wild, staring, not begging, just staring and crying — "Oh, my God . . . not you . . . not *you*. . . ." — And her eyes, two perfect mirrors of his own face —

He'd hated what he'd seen in her eyes.

In that last split second, what he'd seen there with the horror and the terrible fear.

Pity.

He'd shoved her, hard, because he'd *had* to, because she knew who he was now, and she was *sorry* for him, and he *hated* her for that . . . hated . . . "Oh, Donna . . . Donna . . . " he whimpered, "I didn't want to kill you, too . . . "

And again he heard the screams, Donna's screams as her body had hurtled down the cliff, and his screams, even now, as he leaned against the lighthouse wall, and he couldn't stop . . . couldn't stop. . . .

It was all Kelsey's fault.

She had tricked him.

The lifeguard drew a ragged breath and stared down at the limp body on the rocks.

Tricked him. . . .

Now . . . and finally . . . it was *his* turn.

Chapter 21

At first she thought it was still night.

The room was so dark that Kelsey groped for the clock and stared at it, convinced it must have broken sometime while she slept.

The hands read 8:30.

Puzzled, Kelsey roused herself and looked out through the windows. It was hard to tell where the ocean ended and the horizon began. The sky was a boiling mass of black, the waves choppy shadows, the sand gunmetal-gray, so that everything melted together in a thick, murky blur. Sporadic stabs of lightning pierced the clouds, and a strange, thick mist hung over everything. Kelsey shuddered and jumped out of bed, switching on the light. She wouldn't be taking a walk this morning.

There was a radio going downstairs — she could hear the drone of a newscaster and bursts of static. A cabinet door opened and closed. There was a murmur of voices, the smell of strong coffee. The phone rang once, then clattered down again. The boys were probably both downstairs; Kelsey doubted if the beaches would open today.

She went to the closet and rummaged through her sparse assortment of clothes. She hadn't planned on it being quite so cold, and now Donna had borrowed her only jacket. She hoped Donna didn't forget to return it — it was her favorite one. Thinking of Donna now made her smile. She had grown close to her in such a short time — she hoped they would stay friends, even after Kelsey went back home. She chuckled to herself. Hopefully Donna would be recovered now from her fight with Skip, although Skip probably deserved to suffer, just a little.

The jeans and shirt she finally put on weren't nearly warm enough. Kelsey hesitated a minute, staring into the closet at Beth's things. Maybe there was a T-shirt or light pullover she could tuck discreetly under her own shirt. It really was so cold in here. . . .

A quick search through the hangers proved fruitless. Kelsey stood on tiptoe, trying to see the high shelf at the back of the closet. There were stacks of things folded and several boxes — maybe there was something she could borrow.

She dragged a chair over and stood on it. Pulling on the nearest pile of clothes, she was instantly showered with envelopes that fell from a box without a lid.

"Damn!" Kelsey jumped back and began gathering everything up — clippings, photographs, letters — trying not to look at them, feeling like the worst kind of intruder. She had just swept them all back into the box when suddenly one particular piece of paper caught her eye. Unlike the others, this one didn't have an envelope, and it had come unfolded in the fall so that the scrawled writing was clearly visible. But it wasn't only the writing which caught her attention now — it was the official insignia stamped across the top:

BROOKFIELD PSYCHIATRIC HOSPITAL

For several long minutes Kelsey stared at it, and then, hating herself, she began to read, her eyes widening as they descended the paper.

Dear Beth,

Yes, to answer your last letter, I'm doing much better. As you can see, they even let me have a pen to write with now! Doc says I'm making great progress. I've had lots of time to think here — to think about what I almost did. I know you can't run away from your troubles. I'll never be Justin, and Dad will never accept me like he does Justin — I guess I have to live with that. What I tried to do to myself was the worst thing I could ever have done. But I'm lucky — I'm getting a second chance and I want to make it work this time.

So how's Dad? Justin calls, but never comes — the calls are always in secret, of course. Guess I'm not the sort of thing you want your important friends to know about. But I guess I can handle that, too.

*But why hasn't Dad at least been to see
me? Or written? Or anything?*

*I'm glad you liked the scarf I sent. And
you're sweet to keep writing me, to keep
believing in me. Guess you're the only one
who does, besides myself. Maybe if we'd
been born into some different family, you
and I could have known each other better.*

*Time to put this out for the mail. I look
forward to your letters — they keep me
going.*

Neale

P.S.   *I love you, too.*

Kelsey stared.

And even after she refolded the paper and
put it back in its box, she sat there on the floor,
staring but not seeing . . . until finally the
room, and her thoughts, began to focus back.

Neale? In a psychiatric hospital? Her mind
could hardly grasp it, and she shook her head,
incredulous. *Neale . . . and envious . . . of
Justin?* Kelsey stared at the folded paper. What
had Neale tried to do to himself? *Brookfield
Psychiatric Hospital.* Yet there was something
else in the back of her mind . . . something important . . . *Brookfield* . . . something that Donna
had told her. . . .

"Kelsey? You awake?"

The tap on her door brought her to her feet
just as the bedside lamp dimmed and went out.
"Yes, I'm up." Frowning at the sudden gloom,
she stuffed the box back into the closet and

flung open the bedroom door, hoping she didn't look guilty.

Justin didn't seem to notice anything wrong. "The power just went out, and the phones are out, too. We're in for one hell of a storm, I'm afraid."

Kelsey followed him downstairs and saw Skip hunched over on the couch, lighting some kerosene lamps. Judging by his rumpled appearance and grumpy expression, Kelsey guessed he had spent the whole night on that very spot.

"Feeling better?" she asked, and he gave her a sullen look. "Coffee?"

Skip groaned and frowned at the couch. "Is this made out of concrete or what?"

"Concrete," Justin grinned, handing Skip a freshly filled cup. "You've been up for an hour already — I thought you'd have all the kinks worked out by now."

"I'm probably ruined for life."

"You're just nursing a broken heart," Justin said. "These things take time."

Kelsey patted his knee. "Did anyone get ahold of Donna?"

"Yeah, I called her. And called her. And called her. Last night, and this morning, too, till the damn phones went dead. No answer."

Kelsey felt the first nagging twinge of worry. "Should we go and check on her?"

"And give her the satisfaction? You must be joking."

"It's not unusual," Justin informed her, "for Donna not to answer when they've had a fight."

"But *I'd* like to talk to her," Kelsey insisted.

"Good." Skip waved his hand. "You talk to her. Tell her what a brat she's being — "

"Skip — " Kelsey admonished.

"Kelsey — " Skip retorted, "tell her it's her own fault — "

"Skip, aren't you even the least bit upset? And what's this on your neck?"

Skip fingered the wide red welt that encircled his neck, and he frowned. "My chain must have come off last night in the water. Terrific . . . there goes my key again — damn, it feels like a rope burn. Any of you guys have a spare key?"

Justin fumbled at his pockets, his face blank. "Neale must have borrowed mine — Come on Skip, just admit it. You're upset about Donna. I'll just get the jeep and we'll — "

To Kelsey's surprise Skip nudged him roughly aside. "Why should I be upset? I can have anything I want, so why should *I* be upset? She's the one who should be upset — she deserves it." He stomped from the room, throwing a last remark. "She deserved exactly what she got."

Kelsey felt a ripple of fear move up her spine. She looked at Justin, waiting for some explanation, but he only looked as upset as she felt. Without a word he followed Skip into the kitchen, leaving her alone and strangely troubled. *Something . . . something's not right. . . .*

Uneasily Kelsey opened the front door and surveyed the mounting storm. The trees were whipping wildly in the wind — the ocean looked maniacal . . . bursting on the shore, exploding in a black frenzy that chilled her to the bone. *Something . . . something. . . .*

"I'm going to check on Donna," Skip said suddenly behind her. She whirled around, cheered a little by his change of heart. "You wanna come with me?"

She did, but instead shook her head. "No . . . I think three might be a crowd if there's any making up to do."

Skip pondered these words of wisdom, then shook his head. "No, I think maybe you should be there. So when she crawls back and I refuse her, you can arbitrate." He took her punch on his arm and grinned, more like his old self again.

"You might as well go with him," Justin urged, shrugging into his jacket. "Neale's gone off to check something up the beach, and I need to go find him. I'd feel better if you weren't alone."

So you feel it, too, Kelsey thought, and she met Justin's eyes with a slight shock — they seemed to confirm her sense of foreboding. *Something . . . something's not right. . . .*

"Yeah, come on. We'll take the shortcut up by the lighthouse — it'll be faster." Skip propelled her out to his jeep, not giving her time to answer. She gasped as the wind nearly knocked her over, and Skip helped her into the seat, his own body braced against the fierce gusts. "Sit close to me!" he ordered her, and she scooted into his side, glad to have something to lean on.

"I need a jacket!" she shouted, and Skip coaxed the jeep to life, sending them both back against the seat.

"You can get one at Donna's. What do you think *I'm* here for anyway?" He slipped an arm around her and hugged her close, waving smugly to Justin as they started off. Justin waved back and shouted something, but it was lost in the wind.

A clap of thunder shook the air, the sky, splitting the clouds. Kelsey jumped as the rain hit her — not a light sprinkling, but an unleashed torrent that turned the world an instant, impenetrable gray. They were drenched within seconds.

Skip hung over the wheel, squinting through the impossible curtain of rain. "Damn! I can't see a thing out here — "

"I think we're too close to the water, Skip! Maybe we should — " Kelsey began, but she never got to finish her sentence.

For one split second the waterfall around them seemed to part, revealing a long, dark shape sprawled directly in their path, a shape they gaped at, unbelieving, even as they went right over it.

"What the — " Skip fought wildly for control as Kelsey screamed. There was the sickening feel of earth giving way beneath them, and the dizzy sensation of spinning — on and on through the rain —

Kelsey felt herself hurtling through the air
. . . felt the ground smack into her face . . .
heard the crash, somewhere, beneath the
thunder and wind and rain —

"Skip! Skip, where are you?"

The scream stuck in her throat, strangely
metallic; she gagged on it and felt it rush, warm
and thick, down over her chin. Blood. Blood
everywhere.

What did we run over? In horror she tried
to lift her head, spitting out bloody water and
sand. Her whole face felt numb . . . she couldn't
feel her nose at all. . . .

"Skip? Oh, God. . . . "

She tried to crawl then, to drag herself
toward where she had heard those last awful
sounds — but the world was a dark void and
the rain beat down on her, pinning her to the
ground —

"I'm coming, Skip! Hang on!" *Why doesn't
he answer me — why doesn't he call?* "Skip!"
She pulled herself to her knees, her head exploding with pain, and scrambled to her feet
as water sloshed over her wrists. Was she too
near the water, she wondered frantically —
inches from the waves? She had no idea how
far she'd been thrown in the crash — and now
it suddenly occurred to her that Skip wasn't
answering because the jeep had gone into the
ocean —

"Skip!"

It all looked so much alike — water and sky
and sand and rocks — but no, it *didn't*, she told

herself angrily, it *didn't*, it was *fear* making it look that way, and if she could just calm down and get her bearings —

She saw the jeep then. It seemed to leap out of the rain at her, about twenty feet away, and as she stumbled toward it, she saw that it lay uselessly on its side. She drew in her breath, dreading to go any closer.

"Oh, Skip," she said softly, and she was there now, trying to peer underneath, trying to steel herself for what she would find —

She found nothing.

Skip wasn't there.

Startled, Kelsey staggered back. There was nothing but sand and water and storm. She was alone.

Panic engulfed her; she turned in circles, screaming, "Skip! Skip! Where are you?" It was crazy — he *couldn't* have disappeared — it was *impossible!* There was no place to go except the cliffs, and no one with an injury would dare risk the climb, especially in this weather. Kelsey's brain reeled, and she choked back a sob. He couldn't have just left her there — why on earth would Skip just go off and leave her — without making an effort to find her, without calling to see if she was all right. . . ?

Help . . . I've got to go back and get help — She had no idea how far they'd come, how long it would take to get back — she knew Justin and Neale were out somewhere on the beach — if only they would find her, if only they would come — *But I can't wait.* Sick at heart she knew she couldn't take that chance. If Skip were lying unconscious somewhere, his life might depend on her.

Ducking her head into the wind, she tried to run . . . stumbled . . . tried again. Her head was throbbing; her left leg felt pulled at a strange new angle. She shut her eyes and gritted her teeth, pushing herself forward by sheer willpower.

She didn't see the body until she stumbled over it.

Sprawling beside it, she cried out in renewed pain and fear, her mind registering much too slowly as her eyes grazed over the figure face-down in the sand.

"Oh, no . . . Skip — "

But even as she said it, she knew it wasn't Skip.

Even as she said his name . . . even as her hand plucked cautiously at the shoulder, even as she leaned close to heave the body over, she knew with a dreadful certainty that this was the terrible thing that had caused their accident, and that it wasn't Skip at all.

This body was plastered to the sand.

Kelsey gave one last shove and it came loose, flopping over on its back like a weighted rag doll.

At first she thought he was screaming. His mouth was open. And then she saw the yellow teeth, and the tongue swollen twice its size. . . .

And the gaping hole where the eye patch should have been —

And the long red scarf twisted around his neck.

And then she realized that Isaac was quite dead and that the screams were coming from other places — the wind — the sea — the dark caverns of her mind. . . .

Isaac! Her head pounded mercilessly, her chest squeezed in revulsion. *Isaac!* Washed up on shore like all his helpless, innocent victims, and now Kelsey was safe . . . Neale . . . Justin . . . everyone, at last, was *safe.* . . .

In morbid fascination she stared down at the grotesque figure and saw something shiny in one of his hands, something small and blue and shiny, part of it still wedged between his stiff, clawed fingers, as if Isaac, even in death, was loath to give it up.

Curious, Kelsey leaned over and reached for it. *Suppose he's not really dead . . . suppose he grabs me and pulls me into the water and —* Kelsey snatched the object away and jumped back, a frown creasing her brow as she examined the thing in the palm of her hand.

It was a key.

And she had seen it — or one just like it — once before.

Kelsey felt faint, yet she couldn't wrench her eyes from that key. And while the rain pelted her unmercifully, she was suddenly standing in the bright sunshine in a spot not far from this very beach, on another day, defending herself against Neale's anger. . . .

"Only the lifeguards have keys to it. . . ."

Only the lifeguards.

Skip's key had been gone this morning. He'd said he lost it last night in the water . . . diving after the victim that nobody could find. . . .

"Oh, my God," Kelsey whispered. She stared down at Isaac's contorted face, frozen in a cold mask of fear. She remembered how she had struggled with him . . . how terribly strong he had been. . . .

But someone had been stronger.

Someone would have to be stronger to overpower Isaac.

And Isaac must have fought desperately for his life.

Desperately enough to rip a key away without his attacker knowing it . . . desperately enough to rip a key from a chain around someone's neck and leave a burn. . . .

She couldn't believe it.

Kelsey began to cry. For Beth. For herself. For Isaac. "Oh, no . . . no. . . ."

Only the lifeguards.

She saw the shape, then, tall and distorted, a staggering blur through the fog.

He wasn't hurrying. He was taking his time.

". . . *the tracking . . . that's the real fun of it . . . they don't see you . . . but they know they're going to die. . . .*"

"Kelsey!" Skip shouted. "I know you're there!"

And Kelsey ran. . . .

And knew she was going to die.

Chapter 22

She never even considered where she would go.
Panic left her with no sense of direction, and
she raced along the beach in a mindless frenzy.
Where was he now? How close behind her?
Would he kill her first and then throw her into
the sea or —

"No!" she cried, wrestling with twisted,
blood-spattered images, as memory after horrible memory washed over her. Skip's temper,
Skip's jealousy, Skip's ugly threats to Donna —
they were all making sense now. She remembered his candidness with her that night in his
bedroom, the beautiful deer head hung on his
wall surrounded by all those muscle-building
machines — *"I just take it"* — *"I get whatever
I want"* — *"she deserved what she got. . . ."*

". . . they don't see you but they know. . . ."

Kelsey, I think someone is going to kill me.

Beth had known, had suspected all along that
someone was after her. How long had he stalked
her, Kelsey wondered now, waiting for his
chance, enjoying her fear and helplessness,

knowing all along that he would kill her in his own time. . . .

"She trusted you!" Kelsey cried and fell facedown as wind and spray hit her full force. She had to get up . . . get help . . . but it was like trying to wade through quicksand. She could hardly move her legs anymore. How many others had there been, how many girls that no one even knew about? And the murders at Skip's school . . . those nice girls who would never get in a car with a stranger . . . girls that had just disappeared off the face of the earth? So he had satisfied his urges wherever he went. . . .

She heard his footsteps, plodding along behind her.

She pulled herself up and ran for her life.

Isaac had known who the killer was, and now he was dead. And it was her fault. Her fault for telling what she suspected, for trusting Skip, for being so nosy and getting involved. . . . Skip was systematically disposing of all possible witnesses — and if Isaac was dead, everyone would think the mystery was over. Except that she had seen Isaac now, and she knew better, knew that he'd been strangled before his body had ever touched the water. . . .

Skip had played games with her. Twisted, little games of spying and sneaking into her room and listening in on the phone when he'd been next door. Isaac had tried to warn her, and she hadn't believed him. But now Isaac was dead, and she had found him, and she had seen the key.

She knew who the real killer was.

Skip couldn't afford to let her live.

Kelsey stopped with a jolt. The cliffs were high above her, blocking her escape, just as they had prevented escape for so many, many others through all the centuries past. With a cry of terror she veered off, following the base of the incline until at last she stumbled out onto the road.

The road that led up to the lighthouse.

With the gate unchained and open.

Kelsey plunged ahead, dragging herself up the steep rise. She wasn't sure how much longer she could hold out — she couldn't feel anything anymore. Every sound was Skip — Skip bursting out of the rain, out of the fog, out of the shadows, to kill her. Funny, she thought, and had a sudden desire to laugh at the absurdity of it all — Neale had hated Skip all this time, must have suspected him all along — *and I was afraid of Neale. . . .*

"Kelsey!"

She froze.

The scream came out of the rain, not behind her now but above her, and not the same scream, but a different one.

"Kelsey!"

Panting, she stopped. The road, the rocks, everything was deserted. Through the curtain of gray rain she could see the lighthouse like a tall, wavy ghost, and the vague outline of its door at the bottom . . . and the vague black silhouette of someone just inside.

"Kelsey," the voice implored her, full of fear

and pain, "It's Donna — help me — "

Somehow Kelsey made it. Somehow she managed to pull herself the last few yards across the ledge and fall in at the door, exhausted, grateful.

"Donna!" she gasped. "Donna, where are you?"

But the wind had come with her, slithering in through the holes and the cracks, and the only sound that answered was its long, shrill, empty moan.

"Donna?" Kelsey whispered, and her voice throbbed back again in a hollow echo . . . *Donna* . . . *Donna.* . . . She got unsteadily to her feet, looking around in awe.

Most of the floor had rotted away, along with the floors up above. Where Kelsey stood she could look up through broken boards and fallen ceilings, up into the yawning hole of the lighthouse dome . . . the shattered remnants of the old light tower. High above her the rain came in, pattering around her in sharp, tinny drips, making puddles around her feet. Where doorways had once been, groups of small black shapes now clotted over broken beams, and as one of the shapes gave an uneasy stir, Kelsey stepped back in alarm, watching its bony bat wings enfold it once again.

"Donna," she murmured, and her eyes swept the gloom around her, indistinct forms she couldn't quite make out because they loomed so far beyond the pale light. . . .

Light. . . .

Kelsey's heart stopped. Across the room there

was a grimy lantern, spilling light weakly onto the bare rock floor. *Someone was here. . . .*

"Kelsey, help me!"

She whirled at the cry, ice in her veins. "Donna!"

"I'm hurt! I think I've broken my leg — down here!"

Down here . . . but I could have sworn I saw you standing in the doorway. . . . "Where?" A mixture of fear and relief took over, guiding her gingerly over the rocks, making her voice quiver. At least Donna was safe — but what in the world had she been doing in here where she knew no one was ever supposed to be? "Hang on, I'm coming!"

Kelsey picked her way nearer to the lantern. Now she could see the stairwell — or what was left of it — a yawning hole in the floor flanked by a wobbly rail. "What did you do? Fall?" She paused, waiting for an answer, but there was nothing. "Donna?" she called softly.

Picking up the lantern she started down. It was a winding staircase of rusted iron, and with each careful footstep the whole thing threatened to tear away from its shaky bolts. Kelsey strained her ears, forcing her eyes straight ahead, away from the slimy walls and the mold that clung there, the grotesque shadows pulsing around her. Every footfall, every beat of her heart seemed magnified a hundred times. She felt as if she were descending into a grave. "Donna? Please answer me —"

Echoes. She heard echoes, mournful and

empty — wind crying and rain lashing and the soft slurp — somewhere — of water. . . .

Water. . . .

Kelsey's foot plunged down into nothingness.

Screaming, she flung out her arms to catch herself, but the useless bannister twisted beneath her grasp, loosening from the wall with a horrible groan. The lantern swung in a crazy arc, and as Kelsey pitched forward, there was a wide swath of pale light — stone walls — wet rocks — bats — and more bats — squirming restlessly — wings quivering —

She landed hard, the breath knocked out of her, so that all she could do for several long minutes was lie there and stare at the lantern through a haze of agony. Through some miracle the light hadn't gone out. And now she could see the wall, the rocks, the mass of bats, all in their proper, horrid perspectives.

She seemed to be in some sort of cave.

She heard her own breathing, shallow and labored, surrounding her on all sides, as if others breathed with her. There was a horrible stench in the air, like rotten meat. She gagged and put up her hand — felt blood again on her face. Her leg, bent under her, was throbbing unbearably. *My leg.* . . .

"Donna — " she tried to raise herself on her elbow, tried to penetrate the void and find her friend — "Donna, I think I've done the same thing — " She clutched at her knee, flinching, trying not to faint . . . trying to think what to do. . . . "Donna, we were wrong . . . it wasn't

Isaac, it was Skip — we've got to get out of here, do you hear me? Donna, *where are you?*"

But the voice that floated out of the darkness began to laugh . . . like Donna might have laughed. . . .

"Oh, Kelsey . . . Kelsey. . . ." and it sounded so *amused.* . . .

Only it wasn't Donna.

Someone was trying to sound like her . . . but it wasn't Donna. . . .

The voice laughed again, and it was the same laugh that Kelsey had heard once before . . . when she'd been alone that day . . . alone in the lighthouse. . . .

And still the voice laughed.

And laughed. . . .

"Donna can't help you," it said.

Chapter 23

"What have you done with her?" Kelsey shrieked. She struggled into a sitting position, bracing her arms against the cold, damp ground. *How did he get in here? How could he have gotten here without my knowing?* Her own pain and that awful smell rocked the blackness around her.

The lantern cast a circle of sickly light upon the stone. Just beyond that circle, where the light couldn't reach, a pair of shoes squished wetly and stopped.

"Donna!" Kelsey was crying now, out of her mind with fear. "Where is she, Skip? What have you — "

"Kelsey," the voice admonished gently, still that high, singsong voice that was not — could never be — Donna . . . could never be human. "Kelsey, you made me make a very bad mistake . . . giving Donna your jacket the way you did. . . ."

Eyes wide, Kelsey listened, tears streaming

down her face. "Where's Donna? Tell me where she is — "

"I mean, how was *I* supposed to know you weren't wearing your own jacket? And there I was — with the wrong body on my hands — such a terrible waste. . . ." The feet shifted, stirred the shadows, fell silent again.

"But why?" Kelsey tried to move, to back away, but her leg wouldn't hold her. "Why are you doing this?"

"Why?" the voice threw back at her, and it came from all directions, the whole cave resounding with mockery. "But it gives me so much power, don't you see? So much . . . shall we say . . . inconspicuous attention? Why, I can walk right through a crowd and pick out my victim in broad daylight. Talk to her. Make her feel special." The voice grew dreamy. "Take her out and show her a good time. . ." The voice grew sad, "Make her fall in love with me." There was a brief, reflective silence, then it spoke again. "And — this is the funny part — she never even *dreams* that I'm going to kill her . . . never has the slightest clue that I have her life . . . in my hands."

"You don't have to do this! You have everything anyone could want!" Desperately she tried to stand, but slid down again on the slimy rocks. She knew he was watching her, smugly enjoying her struggles, and she backed farther away, farther away from the light.

The feet moved forward. He was trying to keep her in sight.

"But Beth cared about you! She trusted you!"

"She did trust me. But then . . . they all did, really." Another long pause, another touch of sadness. "I didn't want to hurt Beth. But she found out about me, you see, so I had to. I had no choice. Sometimes people really don't, you know."

She was stalling for time, inching her way back, wrapping herself in darkness. Surely the stairs were back here somewhere — if only she could grab hold — pull herself up —

"I don't have a choice *now*, you can see that, can't you? I wanted you to stay here on the island . . . but now you know too much and you might tell, and then they'd put me away. . . ."

The stairs . . . oh, God, please, help me —

"I could just leave you down here, of course," he went on, hesitating at the very brink of the light. "All these underground caves flood at high tide . . . or sometimes . . . in very bad storms." There was a faint breath of laughter. "But you'd suffer too much. Being so afraid. All alone in the water. In the dark. The bats would come. And snakes. And the rats. . . ."

Kelsey fought down a wave of panic. *A little more . . . little more. . . .*

"I like you too much to let you suffer. I'll do it nice and fast. I'm good at it, you'll see."

Her body jolted as the rubber soles squeaked across the rocks, as the tall, slender figure moved out into the yellow light —

"Kelsey," the voice whispered, and the cave was full of him — "you'll never escape me. You're going the wrong way."

She lunged then, into the utter blackness,

hoping against hope that he was wrong, that the stairs were close, and she heard him, running up behind her, felt his hands on her back as she screamed and screamed and threw herself away —

And fell over the body on the floor.

In that split second of horror, Kelsey saw the face — the eyes — gleaming at her from the darkness — the eyes staring at her above the filthy gag, barely alive below the filthy bandage — the matted hair, the dried blood —

"Oh, God — *Beth!*"

Water surged in.

As Kelsey hurtled into black liquid space she felt the ocean close over her. Gagging, swallowing, she tried to surface, felt a hand clamp down on her head, pushing her under, holding her. She kicked and twisted — eyes wide with terror, but everything was black and distorted . . . even her cries . . . her pleas for mercy. . . .

The pressure on her head let up. Bursting to the surface, she gulped once before the hand pushed her down again. She was vaguely aware of noises, muffled and very far away, and all around her the water was churning, black, black bubbles, waves knocking her helplessly back and forth . . . deeper . . . deeper. . . .

Second chance . . . and even in the midst of panic she recognized the irony of it all. *Saved once to drown later.* . . .

"Kelsey. . . ."

From some dream she thought she heard her name, a blurry, garbled underwater sound —

"Kelsey . . . *where are you —* "

Cold air hit her face, shocking her — and hands, on her shoulders now — she couldn't see the face or the eyes, but the hands were there, strong and powerful, and shoulders and a bare chest —

My God, he's in the water with me!

A new terror seized her; she struck out and heard him curse as he wrestled her arms, her nails from his face —

"Kelsey — *Kelsey!*"

And she went icy all over, recognizing the voice now — that deep, emotionless voice that she had feared all along —

She had been wrong.

The murderer wasn't Skip.

It was Neale.

"No!" she shrieked and went down, her lungs filling with water — *Brookfield Murders — Brookfield Psychiatric Hospital* — as Neale let go of her and twisted sharply beneath the water. Something was happening, she could sense it, even though the world was black and wavy and nothing really mattered anymore. . . .

"*Kelsey.* . . ." And the underwater voice again, Death calling for her, guiding her into the deepest, deepest darkness —

Her head broke the surface once more, as arms lifted her shoulders and someone, somewhere, was shouting, and the lantern was there, throwing sallow light across the cave . . . the water. . . .

"Don't struggle," the voice said. "Don't . . . it'll be easier if you don't struggle. . . ."

And there was a roaring, filling her head, a

growing surge of indistinct sound and another shout, muffled, distant. . . .

"Don't . . . struggle. . . ."

Justin. . . . And she could see him now, his eyes, his face, so near . . . his arms going around her . . . "Justin," she gasped, gratefully, desperately . . . *you've come to save me . . . to save my life* . . . his arms around her, so strong, so determined. . . .

His hands . . . around her neck . . . squeezing. . . .

"Don't struggle — "

But she *was* struggling . . . great gasps of air from lungs bursting, and that split second, that tiny instant of realization as strength gave out and water poured in, black and sickening and endless . . . endless. . . .

"Don't. . . ." and Justin's voice was fading, as everything was fading, as her very life was fading . . . ending. . . .

And in her deep, black nightmare she knew she was dying, knew it just as surely as she knew the faraway echo of Skip shouting, and the frenzied thrashings of the ocean reluctant to give up its own. . . .

And then the calm, hollow trickling of water upon a cold, cavern floor. . . .

And the heartbreaking sound of Neale crying.

Chapter 24

The light.

It hurt her eyes, jarring her from a deep cocoon of blissful oblivion, and she drew back from it, whimpering.

"It's okay. You're safe now." The deep voice was very near; it spoke to her softly, and a hand that had been holding hers slid away.

Kelsey blinked several more times at the pale sunlight across her pillow, at the unfamiliar window with curtains pulled wide. She looked around the room, her surroundings beginning to come into focus at last — faded green walls, hospital furniture — and as she groped for her face, she felt the bandage there, and stared in bewilderment.

"You're in the clinic. Do you remember anything?" Neale asked softly.

She found him then, where he'd been sitting beside her, his eyes sunken and bloodshot, his features taut. There was a shadow on his upper lip, and his hair looked like he'd run his hands through it many times. She stared at him, nodding slowly. *Yes . . . now it all came back. . . .*

She felt a lump in her throat and tears slipped down her cheeks. "Justin — "

Neale shook his head, his face drawn. "I tried to pull him out — he kept swimming away from me. . . ."

Despair washed over her, a long, agonizing wave, and she grabbed for his arm. "I saw Beth. . . ."

"I know. They flew her to the mainland — Dad'll be there with her."

"But is she okay? I thought — "

"She's alive, at least," Neale said gently.

"But, Donna — Neale, I think Donna might be down there, too — "

"No, Kelsey, I'm right here."

For the first time Kelsey noticed the two figures standing quietly near the door. Donna, her leg in a cast, moved painstakingly toward the bed on crutches as Skip tried to support her with his arm.

"Oh, Donna — "

The girls' arms went around each other, and they both began to cry.

"Kelsey . . . he tried to kill me. . . ." They clung to one another, and Donna went on brokenly. "He thought I was dead, I guess — he pushed me over the cliff, and I landed on some rocks. I guess I was out for a while, but when I came to again, he was gone and I tried to crawl back to the beach. To warn you — "

Kelsey's heart ached. She hugged Donna close.

"The beach was swarming with people," Donna took a deep breath. "That's when I found out what had happened in the lighthouse — that Skip had gone on for help, and Neale had stayed with you and Beth, trying to keep her alive — "

"It was Neale who gave you mouth-to-mouth," Skip spoke up. "I just stopped your bleeding. No big deal."

In spite of themselves, the girls laughed, and Skip pulled Donna back.

"Come on, I'm taking you home where I can keep an eye on you," he said gruffly. "Before you get yourself in any more trouble." He leaned down and patted Kelsey roughly on the shoulder, his expression solemn. "You're in good hands. Now get some rest."

Kelsey nodded, tried to swallow the lump in her throat. Donna and Skip disappeared into the hall and Neale lowered his face into his hands, his voice surprisingly steady.

"You thought it was me."

"I thought it was everyone," Kelsey said hollowly. "Except Justin." She couldn't look at him, yet she felt his eyes upon her, calmly assessing.

"I could never have hurt Beth — she was the only one who really cared about me. About any of us. The only one in the family who tried to keep us all together. It was Beth who wanted this summer together, not us. Dad adored her, did anything she asked. He never wanted sons ... thought they were too much bother, better to stick them off somewhere so he could get on with his career. Except for Justin — Justin made him proud. Justin made up for all the bother."

209

Kelsey glanced at him guiltily. "I found one of your letters to Beth. While you were in that hospital."

He nodded, a half smile forming on his lips. "She was the only one who ever wrote me. I never heard from Dad — he was too busy being ashamed of me, I guess. And as for Justin . . . well. . . ."

"What . . . were you in for?"

"You make it sound like a prison sentence." He did smile then, much to her embarrassment.

"I'm sorry, I — "

"No, it's okay," he brushed her apology aside. "Not terribly intriguing, I'm afraid. I was depressed, and I didn't know what to do with my messed-up life. The usual stuff. Except I didn't have anyone to talk to . . . so I went kind of crazy. Even thought of doing myself in."

"You tried . . . to kill yourself?"

Another nod, this one regretful. "Stupid. Stupid thing to do. It happens when you think the world's against you. I know better now, of course." He shook his head slowly. "I thought I was the only one with problems. I wish I'd known about Justin. . . ."

"Then *you* didn't suspect him?"

"No. When things kept happening around the island — I thought it might be Skip." He looked so sorry, and Kelsey's eyes blurred.

"And your dad — he didn't suspect anything, either?"

"I guess it's hard to suspect someone who's so perfect. Perfect grades. Perfect looks. Perfect personality." He dropped his eyes, his face sad. "Perfect disguise."

Kelsey was silent a moment. "You were in the same town while he was in school."

"Yes, that was Dad's idea. To ease his guilt. He put Justin there so someone in the family would be close by. Of course," he added almost as an afterthought, "Justin never came. He was too busy — " his look was filled with unspoken horror — "doing other things."

Kelsey felt a chill go through her.

"Cold?" Neale tucked the blankets around her. She was surprised at how carefully he did it, almost tenderly, and she smiled.

"I'm fine. Have you had lots of experience, tucking girls in?" For the first time she saw a blush creep over his cheekbones. He cleared his throat, trying to look unperturbed.

"You're getting kind of personal, aren't you?"

"Well you *did* save my life, after all. How did you find me?"

"It was Skip, really. He found *me* on the beach — he was running around looking for you and told me he'd turned the jeep over, and he was afraid you were wandering around out there with a concussion or something — that he'd seen you through the fog, but you ran from him, and went for the lighthouse. . . ."

Kelsey shut her eyes against the sudden images and turned her head away.

"Your knee's busted pretty bad — and your forehead — but I think you'll make it. Here.

It's probably cold by now, but I got you some tea."

"You're pretty good at this." Their eyes met ... held ... she knew that hers had filled with tears again. "Why ... didn't he kill Beth?"

Neale looked down, not speaking for a long time. Finally he said, "I guess only Justin knows the answer to that. We never will."

An overwhelming emptiness filled her. She stared at his bowed head. "What will happen now?"

His voice was tired but matter-of-fact. "With Skip's pull around here, and his own story about what happened, I don't think there'll be much trouble getting this thing settled."

She nodded, finding it hard to speak. "And what will you tell your dad?"

He hesitated, scanning her face with his eyes. "That it's over," he said quietly. "That it's all finally over."

She felt the tears racing down her cheeks, felt his strong, gentle fingers as she groped across the covers for his hand. "Second chance," she whispered.

And he smiled at her.

"Second chance," he said.

And raised her hand to his lips. . . .

And kissed it.

About the Author

RICHIE TANKERSLEY CUSICK was born and raised in New Orleans, Louisiana, where she grew up with a ghost in her house. She now lives with her husband Rick, a designer and calligrapher, and their cocker spaniel Hannah, just outside Kansas City, Missouri.

Ms. Cusick, writes music and reads in her spare time. She does all her work at a rolltop desk that belonged to a funeral director in the 1800's, and which, she says, is haunted.

MYSTERY THRILLERS

Introducing a new series of hard-hitting action-packed thrillers for young adults.

THE SONG OF THE DEAD by Anthony Masters
For the first time in years "the song of the dead" is heard around Whitstable. Is it really the cries of dead sailors? Or is it something more sinister? Barney Hampton is determined to get to the bottom of the mystery . . .

THE FERRYMAN'S SON by Ian Strachan
Rob is convinced that Drewe and Miles are up to no good. Where do they go on their night cruises? And why does Kimberley go with them? When Kimberley disappears Rob finds himself embroiled in a web of deadly intrigue . . .

TREASURE OF GREY MANOR by Terry Deary
When Jamie Williams and Trish Grey join forces for a school history project, they unearth much more than they bargain for! The diary of the long-dead Marie Grey hints at the existence of hidden treasure. But Jamie and Trish aren't the only ones interested in the treasure – and some people don't mind playing dirty . . .

THE FOGGIEST by Dave Belbin
As Rachel and Matt Gunn move into their new home, a strange fog descends over the country. Then Rachel and Matt's father disappears from his job at the weather station, and they discover the sinister truth behind the fog . . .

BLUE MURDER by Jay Kelso
One foggy night Mack McBride is walking along the pier when he hears a scream and a splash. Convinced that a murder has been committed he decides to investigate and finds himself in more trouble than he ever dreamed of . . .

DEAD MAN'S SECRET by Linda Allen
After Annabel's Uncle Nick is killed in a rock-climbing accident, she becomes caught up in a nerve-wracking chain of events. Helped by her friends Simon and Julie, she discovers Uncle Nick was involved in some very unscrupulous activities . . .

CROSSFIRE by Peter Beere
After running away from Southern Ireland Maggie finds herself roaming the streets of London destitute and alone. To make matters worse, her step-father is an important member of the IRA – if he doesn't find her before his enemies do, she might just find herself caught up in the crossfire . . .

THE THIRD DRAGON by Garry Kilworth
Following the massacre at Tiananmen Square Xu flees to Hong Kong, where he is befriended by John Tenniel, and his two friends Peter and Jenny. They hide him in a hillside cave, but soon find themselves swept up in a hazardous adventure that could have deadly results . . .

VANISHING POINT by Anthony Masters
In a strange dream, Danny sees his father's train vanishing into a tunnel, never to be seen again. When Danny's father really does disappear, Danny and his friend Laura are drawn into a criminal world, far more deadly than they could ever have imagined . . .

GREEN WATCH by Anthony Masters

GREEN WATCH is a new series of fast moving environmental thrillers, in which a group of young people battle against the odds to save the natural world from ruthless exploitation. All titles are printed on recycled paper.

BATTLE FOR THE BADGERS
Tim's been sent to stay with his weird Uncle Seb and his two kids, Flower and Brian, who run Green Watch – an environmental pressure group. At first Tim thinks they're a bunch of cranks – but soon he finds himself battling to save badgers from extermination . . .

SAD SONG OF THE WHALE
Tim leaps at the chance to join Green Watch on an anti-whaling expedition. But soon, he and the other members of Green Watch, find themselves shipwrecked and fighting for their lives . . .

DOLPHIN'S REVENGE
The members of Green Watch are convinced that Sam Jefferson is mistreating his dolphins – but how can they prove it? Not only that, but they must save Loner, a wild dolphin, from captivity . . .

MONSTERS ON THE BEACH
The Green Watch team is called to investigate a suspected radiation leak. Teddy McCormack claims to have seen mutated crabs and sea-plants, but there's no proof, and Green Watch don't know whether he's crazy or there's been a cover-up . . .

GORILLA MOUNTAIN

Tim, Brian and Flower fly to Africa to meet the Bests, who are protecting gorillas from poachers. But they are ambushed and Alison Best is kidnapped. It is up to them to rescue her *and* save the gorillas . . .

SPIRIT OF THE CONDOR

Green Watch has gone to California on a surfing holiday – but not for long! Someone is trying to kill the Californian Condor, the bird cherished by an Indian tribe – the Daiku – without which the tribe will die. Green Watch must struggle to save both the Condor and the Daiku . . .